# Playing Vegas

## PART OF THE HOT VEGAS NIGHTS SERIES

## C.L. COLLIER

# Playing Vegas

## BLURB

A trip to Vegas to celebrate my best friend's wedding?

Yes, please!

I'm ready for warm weather, a little gambling, an epic bachelorette party, and, of course, being a bridesmaid for one of my oldest and best friends.

What I'm not ready for is how hot her younger brother has become. The last time I saw Corey, he was a shy, scrawny kid in high school. Now, he's neither shy nor scrawny, he's a successful business owner, and he's mastered the art of flirting ... mainly with me!

Don't get me wrong—I like having a good time and I'm not opposed to having a weekend fling. But this is my best friend's brother, not a stranger I'll never see again. Should I give into temptation, or play it cool while we're in Vegas?

Cover Design by S.L. Sterling

Editing by Susan Soares, SJS Editorial Services

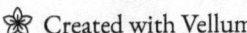 Created with Vellum

*I dedicate this book to all of my fellow romance authors. Let's never stop supporting one another!*

# Brianne

## ONE

"Let's get this party started, bitches!" Dragging my suitcase behind me, I walk toward my friend Olivia, then wrap her in a hug.

"How are you?" she asks.

"I'm great! I had a double espresso at the airport, then a couple of screwdrivers on the plane, so you know, I'm feelin' good." I waggle my eyebrows. "Where's Alex?"

She points over her shoulder toward the baggage claim carousel. "He's waiting for our bags."

I look over her shoulder and see him standing amongst others waiting for their luggage, then back at Olivia. "Have you talked with Chelsea today?"

"No, just the group text this morning telling us where to meet when we get here."

"Same."

Just then, Alex joins us, dragging two suitcases with him. "Hey, Brianne," he says. "Good to see you."

"It's great to see you, too! Should we grab an Uber to the hotel?"

"Let's do it," Olivia replies, and we walk toward the rideshare pickup area.

It's not even eleven a.m. yet, but it feels much later. I arrived at SeaTac at six o'clock this morning to catch my eight o'clock flight. Luckily, my choice of beverages helped wake me up. Not only that, but just being in Vegas is exhilarating. I've been looking forward to this trip for months, not only because we get to celebrate Chelsea's wedding, but I'm overdue for a vacation. I've been putting in more hours than usual at the hair salon, trying to pay off my credit card debt, so this long weekend couldn't come at a better time. Plus, I'm tired of the Pacific Northwest's rainy fall weather. Even though it's November, the weather in Vegas is warm and sunny––just what I need!

"I love how our flights arrived at the same time," Olivia says as we wait for our Uber. "That worked out perfectly!"

"Yeah, it did," I say. "We couldn't have planned it any better." Olivia and Alex flew from Portland, and we were excited when we found out we would arrive in Vegas at the same time without even planning it.

"Are we the last ones to arrive?" Alex asks.

"I think so," I reply. "As far as I know, everyone else has arrived already."

A black SUV pulls up. It's our Uber, so we load our luggage in the back, get in, and then we're on our way to The Caribbean. It's one of the newer hotels located in the middle of the strip, and Chelsea and Carson chose it because of the tropical theme. When they decided to have a destination wedding in Las Vegas and looked at all the options, Chelsea immediately fell in love with the idea of having a wedding in a location that resembled the Caribbean. Their wedding will be outside on the hotel's beach near the impressive pool area. I can't wait to see this place in person; the pictures online looked amazing.

Chelsea, Carson, and their immediate families flew in yesterday. They didn't invite a lot of people to attend their wedding, just their closest friends and family members. Olivia and I are the only non-family members Chelsea invited. The three of us have been friends since middle school, and despite being busy with our own lives and careers now, we're still just as close as we were back then. Olivia doesn't live in Tacoma anymore, but we've managed to keep our bond strong even though she's all the way in Seaside, Oregon. It helps that Alex owns a house in Tacoma, and they visit often.

It's a short ride to The Caribbean. As we pull up to the hotel, it feels as if we're suddenly in a tropical environment. Palm trees and other plants native to the Caribbean line the drive, blocking the view of the strip. If I didn't know better, I could actually be convinced that we're at a resort in a tropical paradise right now, not in the middle of the desert.

Olivia, Alex, and I retrieve our luggage, then make our way into the hotel. As soon as we walk inside, the scent of coconut hits our nostrils, and the sound of reggae music plays on speakers overhead. I'm immediately in love with this place. The lobby is white with several large pots of tropical plants, adding splashes of color. An enormous tank full of tropical fish takes up the entire wall behind the reservation desk. I haven't been to Vegas in a few years, and the last place I stayed was nowhere near as nice as this.

"This is so cool!" Olivia looks around in awe. It seems I'm not the only one impressed with The Caribbean.

As we wait in line to check in, I text Chelsea to let her know we've arrived. She responds right away and lets us

3

know that she's about to get a massage and will see us at lunch, which is on our itinerary for noon.

"Lucky girl. I could use a massage," Olivia says.

"Well, at least you'll get a foot massage after lunch when we get our pedicures," I remind her, referring to our itinerary. Chelsea has provided everyone with a schedule of events for the weekend, starting with lunch today, followed by manis and pedis. Then, later this evening, we'll have the rehearsal, the rehearsal dinner, and then a fun night out to celebrate the last night of Chelsea and Carson being single. They opted to have a co-ed night out, rather than separate bachelor and bachelorette parties.

"That's true. I'm definitely looking forward to that," Olivia says.

"Me, too," I agree. "I'm also looking forward to tonight. I wonder if we'll hit up any strip clubs?"

Alex chuckles. "Is it going to be *that* kind of night out? I figured with everyone going together, strip clubs would be off the table."

I shrug. "Who knows? I'm down for anything, though. You can't go wrong with a night out in Vegas!"

Olivia laughs. "Are you sure about that? You've seen *The Hangover*, haven't you?"

Shrugging again, I reply, "Well, before everything went to shit, those guys had an epic night out. We're smarter than them——we'll be fine."

Olivia laughs again. I'm only half-joking, though. I like to party, and I'm always up for having a good time. I really am up for anything tonight. There's not many things I'm afraid of doing. Out of the three of us, I've always been the more adventurous one. I wasn't afraid to sneak out of my house as a teenager, but Olivia and Chelsea did that maybe once. I was the one who lost my virginity first. I don't deny that I flirted with my high school chemistry teacher to get a passing grade. I've experimented with drugs in the past, and while I'm not proud of everything I've done, I also don't believe in having regrets. My mantra in life is to keep moving forward and do the best I can in life.

Alex and Olivia get called forward to check in, and then I get called forward by another woman working at the counter. Once I'm done and have my room key, I find Alex and Olivia standing to the side, waiting for me near one of the large flower pots filled with beautiful bright pink and yellow flowers.

"What room are you guys in?" I ask as I approach them.

"5072," Olivia says. "How about you?"

"7069," I say with a wide smile. "That's gotta be a lucky number here in Vegas, right? 69?"

Olivia and Alex laugh, rolling their eyes and shaking their heads.

"You crack me up," Olivia says. "But yes, you're probably right."

"So, we're on different floors," Alex says. "I wonder where everyone else is staying?"

"Good question," I say with a shrug. "I guess we'll find out in about an hour, though."

Olivia looks at her watch. "Shall we go to our rooms for a bit and meet up again at lunch?"

"Sounds like a plan," I reply, and we head toward the elevators.

I say goodbye to Alex and Olivia when the elevator stops on the fifth floor, then I continue up to the seventh. Rolling my suitcase behind me, I find my room and hold my key card up to the door to unlock it. When I walk into my room, I'm pleasantly surprised. Not only is the room beautifully decorated, but I have an amazing view of the strip. I didn't realize I paid for a room with a view––maybe I was upgraded––but I'm definitely going to enjoy my stay here.

∼

An hour later, I'm walking into the Caribbean Breeze restaurant where everyone is meeting for lunch. After getting settled in my gorgeous room, I had decided to head down to the casino for a bit. I put twenty bucks into a penny slot and immediately won a hundred dollars! I kept playing, losing a little, then winning a little more, and I ended up cashing out with one hundred forty-eight dollars! Not a bad way to start my weekend in Vegas if I do say so myself!

The restaurant hostess directs me to the large table in the back where I find Chelsea, Carson, and some of their family members. As soon as Chelsea sees me, she wraps me in a hug.

"It's so good to see you, Brianne!"

"This is so exciting! How's everything going so far?"

Chelsea and I let go of one another, and when I see her face, she's all smiles. "So far, so good! Everything is working out just as we wanted. I can't believe this weekend is finally here!"

"I know! It seems like yesterday Carson proposed to you, and now here we are. And I have to say, you picked the perfect location for your wedding."

Just then, Carson walks up and gives me a hug as well. "Hi, Brianne. It's good to see you."

"You, too, Mr. Groom," I say, patting him on the back.

Carson puts his arm around Chelsea and kisses her on the cheek. "Have you seen Olivia and Alex yet?" he asks.

"Yeah, our flights arrived at the same time, and we shared an Uber here. They should be down any minute." I lean in and put my hand to my mouth like I'm telling them a secret. "They're probably putting their room to good use, if you know what I mean."

Chelsea and Carson laugh.

"What's so funny?" I hear Olivia's voice next to me before I turn and see her and Alex.

"Oh, you know, Brianne was just speculating on where you two were," Carson says.

Looking at Olivia, I shrug.

Olivia raises an eyebrow. "Did you think we were having sex?"

Waggling my eyebrows, I reply, "Well, were you?"

Olivia and Alex laugh but don't say anything.

"Oh, I see you blushing," I egg them on.

Olivia shakes her head. "Only you, Brianne," she says with a laugh.

I shrug again, and then Carson changes the subject.

"So, um, guys," Carson says, looking at Alex and Olivia. "I know this is going to be awkward, but Taylor and Wayne are going to be here."

My eyebrows shoot up in surprise, and when I look at Olivia and Alex, they have the same surprised looks on their faces.

"Are you serious?" Olivia asks.

Carson nods. "Yeah. She texted me last night and said she was sorry for everything that happened between us, and she doesn't want to miss my wedding. They're flying in tomorrow."

Alex runs his hand through his hair. He must be nervous as hell now. Long story short, Carson's sister Taylor is Alex's ex-girlfriend. Their relationship ended years ago, and it was quite a shock when Olivia introduced Alex to us, only to discover he and Carson already knew each other from before. To make an even longer story short, Carson and Taylor had a falling out, and she said she wouldn't attend his wedding. I guess she had a change of heart.

"Well, I guess you could say this puts a damper on this weekend," Alex says with a nervous laugh.

"I don't want you to feel uncomfortable," Carson says. "Honestly, Taylor and Wayne are the ones who should feel uncomfortable when they arrive. They've barely spoken to anyone in the family, including my parents in the past couple of months. I think they're using our wedding as an excuse to come to Vegas."

"Not that they need an excuse," Chelsea adds. "They have enough money, I'm sure they can travel whenever they want."

The sound of silverware clanging against a glass gets our attention. We turn and see Chelsea's dad holding a wine glass in the air.

"Good evening, everyone," he says, addressing everyone in our party. "Cheryl and I are glad you could all make it to Chelsea and Carson's wedding this weekend. Please have a seat so we can get the first of many festivities underway!"

We all find seats. Olivia sits to my right with Alex on the other side of her, and Chelsea sits to my left with Carson on her other side. Once everyone has taken their seats, Chelsea's dad gives a short speech, thanking everyone for being here and congratulating his only daughter on her big day. He also praises Carson for being everything he ever hoped his daughter would find in a partner. It's a touching speech, and it even brings a tear to my eye, which isn't easy to do. I don't usually get emotional about things, but there is something about the words Chelsea's dad says that gets to me. Who knows.

The server comes around and takes our drink orders, and I order a dragon fruit margarita. I've never had one before, but I'm all about trying new things, and it sounds delicious.

And it *is* delicious. Two margaritas later and full of food, everyone in our party gets up to leave. Chelsea says goodbye to Carson, who's going to the casino with his buddies while we get our nails done. Chelsea, Olivia, Chelsea's mom, and Carson's mom all walk together to the hotel's salon. I'm feeling good after having two margaritas, but I'm not drunk. I may like to party, but I've learned to pace myself. In my early twenties, I would get out of control pretty easily. Now at the age of twenty-seven, I've matured.

But I still like to have a good time.

The pedicure is relaxing as fuck. Not only does the massaging chair feel good, but the foot and leg massage feels amazing. The glass of champagne they give each of us doesn't hurt either. I'm so relaxed, I could almost fall asleep. Everyone else seems to be enjoying it just as much as I am.

"Chelsea, your brother texted me," Chelsea's mom Cheryl says. "He said his flight was a little delayed, and he just boarded the plane about a half hour late. He's hoping to be here in time for the rehearsal, but he might miss part of it."

"Okay, that's cool. He doesn't have a huge part in the wedding anyway, so it's not a big deal if he misses it."

"What is his role in the wedding?" I ask. I know that Olivia and I are her only bridesmaids, and Carson has chosen his two best friends to be his groomsmen.

"He's going to walk Mom down the aisle," Chelsea

replies. "So, as long as someone tells him when to start walking, and Mom tells him when to stop, he'll do just fine."

"What's Corey been up to lately, anyway?" I ask. I haven't actually seen Chelsea's brother since he was still in high school. He's two years younger than us, and I still think of him as the scrawny little kid who used to try to bother us whenever we went to Chelsea's house. The last time I saw him, he was a senior and still pretty scrawny. He was always a little nerdy... never into playing sports, although he did run track and cross country, and he played the trumpet in band. If I remember correctly, he was on the honor roll, too. So was Chelsea, actually. I definitely never made the honor roll. I was lucky just to graduate.

"He took over our Uncle Garret's construction company last year," Chelsea replies. "He's putting his business degree and expertise in construction to good use. He worked for Uncle Garret's company every summer all the way through college, and after he graduated, Garret hired him full time. He trained him to take over someday, which ended up being about a year ago."

"Wow. Good for him." I have to admit, I'm impressed that Corey is so successful at the ripe young age of twenty-five. I was that age when I decided to go to beauty school. However, I guess it runs in Chelsea's family. She got her teaching degree and started teaching right out of college.

"You probably won't recognize him," Chelsea says with a laugh. "He's bulked up quite a bit since high school."

I can't quite imagine skinny Corey as overweight. "Really?" I scrunch my nose, confused by what she means.

"Yeah, between working construction and lifting weights, he's pretty buff now."

Okay, now *that's* surprising. I can't really picture Corey

with a fit bod, either. Now I'm really interested to see what grown-up Corey looks like.

After our manis and pedis, Olivia, Chelsea, and I decide to hit up the casino for a bit. I'm hoping my good luck streak continues... and I'm not disappointed! By the time we call it quits, I'm up another hundred bucks! After that, the three of us head up to our rooms to refresh before the rehearsal. We have quite an evening ahead of us with dinner afterward, then the co-ed "last night out." I can't wait to see what kind of fun we're going to have out on the strip! I have a feeling this is going to be one epic trip to Vegas.

# *Corey*

## TWO

Vegas. The last time I was here was with my buddies to celebrate graduating college. That was over two years ago. What a crazy trip that was. I'm sure this one will be a bit tamer considering it's to celebrate my sister's wedding. I doubt we'll step foot in a strip club, which is where we ended up every night on that infamous trip.

"The Caribbean?" the older gentleman driving my Uber asks as I get in his car.

"Yes, please," I reply, reaching for my seatbelt. This car is nice--a newer model BMW. It's a car I'd love to buy for myself one day. It's a lot sleeker and more comfortable than my work truck.

I relax in my seat as the driver heads toward the strip. It's been a long day. Hell, it's been a long year. Ever since I took over my uncle's construction company, my life has been beyond busy. Don't get me wrong, I love that my uncle entrusted me with the company he built from the ground up, and I love what I do. But I'm also overworked and in need of a vacation. Most people my age have entry level jobs while I'm running a construction company that runs million-dollar projects. It's stressful, to say the least.

My phone vibrates, notifying me of an incoming text. I look at the screen and roll my eyes. She won't leave me alone. I don't want to be a dick, but I also don't want to lead her on. I never should've gone out on a second date with her. While she's nice, and we get along fine, she's just not my type. I barely have time to date as it is, and I'm becoming more and more picky about the women I want to spend my time with. I may only be twenty-five, but I'm not in college anymore either. I want more than just a good time. I'd like to settle down someday, like my sister Chelsea. She was already in a relationship with Carson when she was my age, and now they're about to get married. I want to be more selective with the women I date because you never know if she'll be the one.

I stare at the text, contemplating how I can let her down easy. She wants to know if I can meet for drinks when I get back to town. I decide to use work as an excuse. I'll just keep doing that––saying I'm too busy with work. She'll get the hint eventually, and honestly, it's not even a lie.

Looking out the window, the hotels on the strip welcome me with their flashing lights and billboards. It's dusk, so it's not completely dark out yet. Chelsea's rehearsal has already started. At least my part in the wedding is easy. I think I can walk Mom down the aisle without practicing first. By the time I get checked into the hotel and put my luggage in my room, the rehearsal dinner will just be starting. I'm thankful I'm not going to miss that––I'm starving!

The driver pulls into The Caribbean's drive. This place was still under construction when I was here last. It's crazy how it looks like I've actually arrived in the tropics. Hope-

13

fully, the hotel rooms are as nice as they looked online. The place my buddies and I stayed was a little sketchy, and I'd never stay there again... but it was all we could afford at the time.

I thank my Uber driver, get out of the car, and retrieve my luggage from the trunk. Then, I make my way into the hotel, which is already a hundred times nicer than the dump I stayed at before. Not that I didn't expect it to be, but the memory makes me chuckle.

As I wait in line to check in, I text Mom to let her know I've arrived. She replies, saying the rehearsal just ended and to meet them at the restaurant for dinner in twenty minutes. I let her know I may be a few minutes late, depending on how long it takes for me to check in and take my bags to my room. I consider having the bellhop take my bags for me, but I'd like to freshen up a bit before going to dinner.

I'm only five minutes late when I walk into the restaurant. The hostess directs me to where the party is, and as I walk up into the private dining room, my mom spots me right away.

"Here's my baby boy!" Mom says loudly, gaining everyone's attention as she walks toward me with her arms wide open.

I chuckle as I give her a hug. "Hi, Mom."

"I'm so glad you're here!" She lets go of me but keeps one hand on my back as she leads me into the room, introducing me to everyone I don't already know.

After meeting everyone on Carson's side of the family, I finally get a chance to say hi to Chelsea and Carson. "I saved you a seat next to me," Chelsea says as everyone takes their seats.

I recognize Chelsea's friend Olivia, who introduces me

to her boyfriend Alex. Then, just as I'm about to take my seat, I look up and see my sister's other best friend, Brianne, across the table from me.

Brianne Hamilton. The girl who made an appearance in several of my fantasies and wet dreams when I was young. I had a crush on her for years, but she was off limits. Not only was she one of my sister's best friends, but she was also a whole two years older than me. Two years seem like nothing now, but back then, it was a big deal.

And holy fuck. Brianne is still beautiful as ever.

"Jesus Christ, *this* is Corey?" Brianne blurts out when she sees me.

Ah, yes. Brianne was also Chelsea's *loud* friend.

She rounds the table and wraps her arms around me in a friendly hug. "It's good to see you!" She pulls back and looks me up and down. "Damn," she says, squeezing my biceps. "You're not a scrawny teenager anymore." She winks, then drops her arms and laughs off her comment. "I'm kidding. Well, kind of. You look good, Corey!"

"Thanks," I say, smiling shyly at Brianne. "You look good, too."

Her lips lift in a smile, and for a split second, I feel as if there may be something in the way Brianne is looking at me. But the moment is over quicker than it happened when she turns and goes back to her chair directly across from my seat at the table.

"Have a seat," Chelsea says, and I notice everyone else doing the same. I look across at Brianne, and she's eyeing me again.

"God, when was the last time I saw you?" she asks. "I know you were still in high school."

I nod. "Yeah, that was a long time ago."

She smiles, then turns toward Chelsea. "You were right. I wouldn't have recognized him."

Chelsea laughs. "He's grown up a lot. He's like a real adult now."

"Hey," I say, nudging my sister with my elbow. "I'm twenty-five, for fuck's sake. Just two years younger than you."

"I know, I know," Chelsea says with a roll of her eyes. "You'll always be my little brother, though."

It's my turn to roll my eyes, but it's all in good fun. I love my family, and I know this weekend will be a ton of fun. I'm happy for my sister and Carson and being in Vegas is a bonus. Not only that, but I can tell Brianne is a spitfire. I remember her being a little wild in high school, and there were a few times my parents weren't sure if Chelsea should hang out with her anymore. It was as if Olivia was her sweet and innocent friend, and Brianne was the troublemaker.

I was just the younger brother back then, but I think Brianne will be a lot of fun to hang out with now. I guess I'll have the chance to find out tonight.

Dinner goes off without a hitch. The food is delicious, and Carson's dad gives a nice speech before dessert is served, thanking everyone for coming. As we begin to eat the creme brulee that is served to us, I ask the question I've been waiting to ask all night. "So, what's the plan for the big night out?"

"Good question, Corey," Brianne says. "What's on the agenda, Chels?"

I smile at Brianne before turning my attention to Chelsea again.

"Well, Carson and I thought we'd start at that ice bar across the street."

"Ice bar?" I ask, not sure what she means by that.

Chelsea nods. "Yeah, it's this bar where everything is made of ice!"

"It's called Arctic Bar," Carson chimes in.

"Even the glasses your drinks are served in are ice," Chelsea continues. "It's so cold inside, they provide you with a parka and gloves to wear!"

I have to admit, that sounds intriguing. "Cool. What's the plan after that?"

She glances at Carson, who says, "There's a burlesque show we thought would be fun to see."

Now we're talking. "Sounds like a plan."

"I like the sound of that," Brianne says. "I love a good burlesque."

I look at Brianne again, and she winks at me. *Damn, she's sexy.*

We finish eating, then everyone gets up from the table and says good night to each other. Chelsea, Carson, Carson's friends and their girlfriends, Olivia, Alex, Brianne, and I are the ones going out to celebrate. There are ten of us altogether, and Brianne and I are the only single ones. We head out of the restaurant together, then walk through the casino toward the exit. The Arctic Bar is located in the Scarlett Hotel & Casino across the street.

As we walk down the sidewalk, I can't help but find myself admiring Brianne. She's outgoing, vivacious, and funny as hell. I can tell she's the life of the party, and tonight will be even more fun simply because she's with us.

When we arrive at Scarlett, we find our way to the Arctic. I've never seen anything like this before--we have to check in with a hostess first, who provides us with a parka and gloves to wear so we stay warm inside. She explains that the bar is kept at subzero temps to keep everything frozen. Everything inside is made of ice, including the bar itself!

After we suit up in our arctic wear, the hostess leads us inside. Aside from it being cold and having ice everywhere, it's kind of like a regular bar. The lights are low, but colored lights glimmer off the ice sculptures throughout the room, making an ethereal experience. There's music playing and a couple of bartenders behind the large chunk of ice sculpted into an actual bar. The only things *not* made of ice are the floor and chairs available to sit on.

"This is awesome!" Chelsea beams. "Let's get a group photo!"

Carson asks another person if they'll snap the photo for us, then we all gather together. Brianne stands at my side, putting her arm around me. I look at her and smile at her beautiful brown eyes as I wrap my arm around her waist.

"Hey, handsome," she says with a sly smile. My cock twitches. If Brianne is going to be flirtatious with me, I'm going to turn up my game as well.

"Smile!" the guy taking the photo says.

Brianne and I both turn our attention and pose for the picture. The guy snaps a couple, then hands Carson's phone back to him. We all move apart from each other, and I have to admit it stings a bit that Brianne immediately moves toward Chelsea and Olivia, leaving me in the dust. Maybe she's not really flirting with me. Maybe that's just her personality.

Our group migrates toward the bar to get drinks. I find myself as the loner of the group. Not that everyone is ignoring me, but everyone has their friends or significant other, while I'm just Chelsea's brother. It's all good, though. I drink my Jack and Coke out of a glass made of ice and enjoy the atmosphere. Our group is having a fun time together, and although I'm the odd one out, I'm still enjoying myself.

My hopes of flirting with Brianne seem to have flushed away as she sticks with the girls, though. We catch eye contact a few times, but her attention always gets pulled back to something else. The more I watch her, the more I find myself attracted to her. It's like I'm a teenager again, and just like back then, Brianne Hamilton is out of my league.

More people come into the Arctic Bar, and the place gets pretty crowded. As I finish my second Jack and Coke, Chelsea announces to our group, "The burlesque show starts in thirty minutes, so we should head over there."

Everyone quickly finishes their drinks, and then we leave. As we exit the bar, we have to stop to return the gloves and parkas. Just as I hand mine to the hostess, Brianne appears at my side.

"It's weird to see you drinking alcohol," she says.

I chuckle. "Is it?"

She nods. "You're Chelsea's little brother. I know we're all grown up now, but it's still weird to me for some reason."

Great. Just what I want––Brianne to still think of me as Chelsea's little bro. I need to squash those thoughts immediately if I ever want to have any sort of chance with her.

Turning on my charm, I lean in and wrap my arm around her shoulder as we walk behind the rest of the group. "Well, you've got one thing right. I'm definitely all grown up now."

"Oh, is that right?" she asks, her voice sounding more flirtatious than before.

I chuckle as I drop my arm from her shoulder. "I may be

Chelsea's younger brother, but there's nothing little about me anymore."

I think I've stunned her. Brianne stops in her tracks, but I keep walking, trying to play it cool. It's uncommon for Brianne to be quiet, but she's speechless. I turn my head to see if she's still walking with us, and she is, just a few steps behind me. I'm not sure if I scared her away or if she's contemplating her next move. I guess I'll find out eventually. The night is still young.

# Brianne

## THREE

H oly shit. Corey telling me there's nothing little about him anymore has me tongue tied. His words have literally stopped me in my tracks, and I have to catch my breath before following the group. It's not like me to not have a comeback after a comment like that––hell, I can think of a few things to say to keep up the flirty banter with him––but this is *Corey*. I've known him since we were kids, and I've *never* found myself attracted to him until tonight. He's always just been Chelsea's little brother. He was that annoying little kid who tried to play pranks on us or tattled on us when we annoyed him. I never expected him to be as hot and sexy as he is now––he's definitely had a glow-up since the last time our paths crossed.

I catch up to the group and walk alongside Corey. We're behind everyone else, with Chelsea and Carson leading the way through the casino. Corey glances at me and smirks.

"You okay?" he asks.

"Uh, yeah. I'm just trying to accept the fact you're not a teenager anymore."

He chuckles. "Yeah, well, neither are you."

*What's that supposed to mean?*

"Is that right?" I ask, hoping he'll elaborate.

He shrugs. "Do you still live in Tacoma?"

His sudden change in topic takes me by surprise. "Yes. Do you?"

"No. I moved to Auburn, closer to work."

"Well, that's not far from Tacoma," I say. "Chelsea said you took over your uncle's construction company. Do you like it?"

"Yeah, I do. It's crazy busy, but I like the fast pace, and business is good."

Everyone stops walking as we reach the theater where the burlesque show is held. We join the line to get in, and Corey and I stay in the back together.

"That's awesome," I continue. "I think it's important to love what you do. That's why I became a hair stylist."

Corey's eyes light up. "That's right. I remember Chelsea mentioning that you do her hair. You obviously do a great job."

I smile at his compliment. "Thank you."

The line moves forward, and we follow the pack.

"So, you've been to a burlesque show before?" Corey asks.

Waggling my eyebrows, I reply, "I sure have. Have you?"

He shakes his head. "Nope. Is it different from a strip club?"

I can't help but smirk at Corey. He's adorable. "The dancers don't get totally naked. But they're certainly entertaining and suggestive." I pause, contemplating whether to say the next thing on my mind. What the hell––why not?

"I'm game for going to a strip club after this. If it's anything like the last burlesque show I saw, it'll be a total turn on."

Corey's speechless as he just looks at me for a second before his lips curl into a mischievous smile. "Is that right?" He leans closer to me and says in a quieter voice, "Do strip clubs turn you on?"

I smile back at him. "Definitely," I say, my voice barely above a whisper.

Corey straightens his posture, clears his throat, and looks straight ahead at the line. "Damn," he says before turning to look at me again. His piercing-blue eyes dance with playfulness, and my stomach flip flops at the sexiness Corey exudes. "I think we'll have to find a strip club after this."

My heart races at the thought of watching strippers with Corey. The thought turns me on, and as we move forward in line once more, I feel a rush of adrenaline. Corey McDonald is flirting with me––and he's good at it. He's no longer Chelsea's younger brother, he's becoming my crush. Maybe I'll get lucky this weekend... I wouldn't be opposed to having a little fun. The only problem is this is my best friend's brother. How would she feel about me hooking up with him?

As we enter the theater, our flirting is put on hold as our group figures out where our seats are located. It's an intimate theater, and all seats are around tables. Our group has to sit at three different tables, since there are four chairs at each one. Chelsea, Carson, Olivia, and Alex sit at one together, while Carson's friends and their girlfriends sit at another. That leaves only Corey and me to sit at the third table together, and butterflies immediately take off in my belly. No one else is sitting in the other two chairs at our table, and

I wonder if anyone will. Corey and I might end up sitting alone together.

A cocktail waitress dressed in a skimpy, sparkly dress asks what we'd like to drink. Corey orders a Whiskey Sour, while I order another White Russian. I've learned over the years to stick to the same drink––or at least the same alcohol––to avoid a hangover.

The lights are low in the theater, and soft jazz plays over the sound system as people continue to find their seats. Still, no one sits next to us.

"Well, this should be fun," Corey says, leaning in close to me. "It looks like it'll just be you and me sitting together."

I smile. "It appears that way. Are you ready for this?"

"Oh, I definitely am. Are you?"

"I'm more than ready," I say just as the cocktail waitress returns with our drinks.

The overhead lights turn off as the stage lights go on. The crowd erupts in applause and whistles, waiting for the show to start, and then the slow, sexy music starts. Taking a sip of my drink, I try to relax in my seat. As the dancer takes the stage, stepping out in a short 1920s flapper-style dress, my body is fully aware of Corey's presence just inches away from me. It's as if I can feel electricity pulsing between us. As the dancer's moves become more provocative, that electric pulse intensifies.

"She's fucking sexy." Corey startles me, whispering in my ear, his breath sending a tickle down my neck.

I turn to look at him. "Yeah, she is," I reply with a wink.

Corey smirks, then leans in close again. "Do you like watching women?"

I bite my lip. "I do find women sexy. I like men, too, though."

Corey smiles. "Are you bi?"

Leaning a bit closer to him, I confess, "I guess I am a little." Then I turn back toward the stage.

The dancer on stage is now wearing nothing but pasties over her nipples, along with a pair of boy short-style panties. She really is sexy, and I'm turned on by watching her. Her breasts are perky, and the tassels on her pasties bounce about as she continues to dance. She ends her routine by going down into the splits, and the crowd goes wild. Before the cheers die down, another dancer takes the stage, wearing an outfit I can only describe as an old Vegas showgirl style. She steps over the other girl, still holding the splits on the floor, and she looks up at the showgirl dancer. The showgirl caresses the other's cheek, then takes her hand to help her up. The first dancer flaunts around the second one on stage, stopping behind her. Then, she rips the showgirl costume off the other girl, leaving her wearing nothing but a sheer, sparkly leotard that makes her look as if she's naked.

The first dancer leaves the stage, and we watch as the new one slinks around sexily. Her leotard is slightly transparent, so when the spotlight hits her breasts head on, you can see her taut nipples through the material.

I really am turned on by these girls. And I didn't exaggerate or lie to Corey just to shock him. I do find women sexy, and I don't consider myself to be totally straight. While I've never had a relationship with a girl, and I only date men, I have had a couple of sexual encounters with women before.

I finish my White Russian, and I feel myself on the edge of being drunk. I've had five drinks tonight including the ones I had at dinner, then at the Arctic Bar, and now here. The dancer finishes her routine, and then our cocktail waitress reappears, asking if we want another. Both Corey and I do, so she retreats to the bar to put in our order, and we turn our attention to the stage again, where two more dancers are starting another dance.

I look at everyone else in our party, sitting at the other tables near us. They all look as though they're enjoying the show. I wonder what we'll do after this. When we talked about tonight's plans, nothing else was mentioned after the burlesque show. It won't be super late, so I wonder what everyone else will want to do. Maybe a dance club? That would be fun––especially being on a crowded dance floor with Corey. I wouldn't mind rubbing my body against his....

I cross my legs, trying to get some relief. Just thinking about grinding against Corey on a dance floor turns me on but combined with watching two practically naked women dance together on stage right now, my clit now throbs.

Then, I remember Corey mentioning a strip club, and the thought of going to one with him turns me on even more. Imagining getting a lap dance together ... having a beautiful, naked woman grinding against both of us ... *holy shit*, I need to stop fantasizing and get a grip on my libido. This is *Corey* I'm thinking about! My best friend's brother! How can I possibly have these kinds of thoughts about him?

One thing that's always been true, though, is that once I get something in my head, I can't let it go. I know this might be risky, but I also know I'm willing to take that risk. My attraction to Corey is strong, and I can tell he's attracted to me, too. We're in Vegas––the City of Sin. Why not enjoy this trip and have a little fun?

After the show ends, we make our way out of the theater. All ten of us gather around, unsure of where our evening will take us next.

"Let's go to a dance club," Chelsea suggests, and everyone agrees.

"I know where to go," Carson's friend Bryan says. "There's a dance club just down the street from here that's amazing."

"Let's go!" Chelsea says as she takes Carson's hand and walks toward the exit. The rest of us follow, and once again, Corey and I wind up behind everyone else in the group, walking side by side.

"That was fun," he says. "Those dancers were amazing."

"Yeah, they were." It's weird to make small talk now after our conversation had gotten so intimate earlier.

"Are you ready to do some dancing now?"

I look at Corey. "You bet I am. Are you?" I cock an eyebrow, hoping we get back to flirting.

"I want to watch you dance." His words are quiet so only I can hear them.

My heart rate picks up again. "Is that right?"

He nods, then looks away and chuckles.

"What's so funny?"

He looks at me again and smiles. "Nothing. I'm just looking forward to this."

We follow everyone outside and walk toward the strip. Nothing else is said between Corey and me because Olivia and Chelsea break away from their guys, so all of the girls walk together, and the guys are leading the way. Corey looks back at me with a cocky smile, and my belly muscles clench. God, he's sexy. How did I never find him attractive when we were younger?

"I haven't gone to a dance club since college," Jolene, Aaron's girlfriend, says.

"Oh, this one's fun," Bryan's girlfriend Sasha says.

27

"Bryan and I came to Vegas about a year ago and loved this place."

All of us are obviously buzzed, if not drunk already. I'm still teetering between the two. The walk to the dance club takes longer than I expect, even though it's only a couple of blocks away, but we finally arrive. The music is loud, thumping all the way out on the street, and there's a line of people waiting to get in.

"Ugh, there's a line," Chelsea says.

"Don't worry about that," Bryan says as he leads us straight up to the bouncer at the door. I can't hear what he says, but he talks to the guy for a moment before the bouncer nods and lets us in.

"Holy shit," I say, stunned that he's able to get us in ahead of everyone else. I look at Sasha. "What did he say?"

She shrugs. "Who knows. He's good at getting into places."

Wow, I'm impressed with Bryan.

As we walk into the club, the music pounds through my body. The dance floor is packed. As I look around, I see there are three levels to this place. The second and third floor have balconies that look down at the dance floor in the middle of the main floor. It looks like there are VIP tables on the second floor, and more people are dancing on the third.

We make our way to the bar, which is crowded with people. The guys are ahead of us, and I'm surprised when Corey shows up in front of me, holding a drink in each hand.

"Here," he says, handing me one of the drinks. "I got this for you. Vodka and cranberry juice."

Smiling, I take the drink from him. "Thank you."

"I know you were drinking vodka earlier, so I stuck with that. I hope you like it."

I take a sip through the straw, keeping my eyes on Corey the whole time. He watches me with heat in his eyes. I swallow, then say, "It's delicious."

"Come on, guys!" Chelsea says as she passes us to go out to the dance floor.

We follow her and everyone else onto the floor. It's crowded, so Corey and I have no choice but to be close to one another. Olivia and Alex are on the other side of me, and the rest of our party is nearby as well. I move with the music, and I'm taken by surprise when Corey puts his hand on my hip.

A sly smile is splayed on his lips as we move together to the music. Holding my drink in one hand, I set the other on his hip as well. I'm impressed that Corey can dance so well, a thought I always used to have when I frequented dance clubs crosses my mind––men who can move their hips this well on the dance floor also perform well in bed.

For a while, it feels as if Corey and I are the only ones here. We look into each other's eyes as we dance. The music vibrates through my body but also pulsates between us, pulling us closer together.

But then Chelsea is at my side. "Come with me," she says in my ear, then drags me off the dance floor.

Olivia is with her, and she takes me near the bar, where there's a spot for us to actually stand away from others.

"What's going on with you and Corey?" she asks.

Shit.

"We're just having fun," I say, shrugging my shoulders. "You don't need to worry."

"Brianne," Chelsea says. The tone of her voice reminds

me of my mom's when I was a teenager, and she didn't believe what I was telling her.

"What?" I ask, not sure where she's going with this. Is she mad? I can't tell.

Her eyes squint. "I think you should know that Corey tends to get around ... if you know what I mean. Just be careful and don't expect too much."

I burst out laughing. Did she forget who she's talking to? Maybe she should have this conversation with her brother and warn him about *me*.

I calm myself and look at my friend again. "We're just having fun, Chels. We're the only two single people in the group. Do you want me to stay away from him?"

Chelsea scrunches her nose. "No, I didn't mean that..." She looks flustered, like she's not sure what she wants to say. Finally, she blows air out of her mouth, then shakes her head. "You guys are both adults and can do what you want. Honestly, I know both of you have a lot in common and would probably get along great. I just wanted you to know about Corey's past. He's kind of a player."

Smiling at my friend, I put my hand not holding my drink up and point my finger at myself. "Hello? Who's the player here? Seriously, there's no need to worry."

Chelsea gives me a hug, then I turn and give Olivia one as well. "Have fun," she says in my ear.

As we walk back toward the dance floor, I spot Corey dancing with another girl. *Damn.* An unexpected feeling of jealousy overwhelms me, and I wonder if Chelsea's words were actually valid. Maybe I *do* need to be careful.

And then another thought crosses my mind. Am I really the same girl I used to be? Do I still *get around*? Sure, I've had more one-night stands than I've had relationships in my life, but it's been quite a long time since that's happened. Is that who I really am? Is that who I *want* to be?

Corey's eyes meet mine, and he grins, lifting his drink in the air. I lift mine as well, then follow Olivia and Chelsea to dance with them instead. If he wants to dance with someone else, go ahead. So, we flirted and had a few moments tonight ... I don't need Corey to have fun, especially if he'd rather have fun with someone else.

# Corey

## FOUR

W ell, fuck. That didn't go as planned.

When Brianne followed Chelsea and Olivia off the dance floor, this chick turned around and danced with me. I didn't want to be a dick, so I danced with her. I figured when Brianne returned, I'd casually move away from this girl and go back to the one I really want to dance with.

But Brianne saw me dancing with this chick and didn't come back to me. She followed Chelsea and Olivia instead, and now here I am, stuck dancing with this girl I don't want to dance with.

I smile kindly at the girl, then turn around to leave. There are so many people on the dance floor, I don't even see where Brianne went. Once I spot her, I make my way through the crowd toward her. She doesn't notice me until I'm literally right in front of her. Her eyes meet my chest, then her head bobs up to look at my face.

"Oh, hey," she says loudly over the music.

I put my hand around her waist to dance with her again. "Are you avoiding me?" I say in her ear.

She shakes her head. "No. You looked busy."

"No, I was waiting for you to come back."

She smiles at me. Maybe it's the alcohol, but I feel the urge to kiss her. Brianne is beautiful, and I'm on cloud nine dancing with her. This is my teenage fantasy come true.

I don't kiss her, though. I'm not about to kill my fantasy as quickly as it's started.

Brianne and I continue dancing, our bodies moving in sync together. When we finish our drinks, I go to the bar to get us another. The more we drink, the more we grind against each other. My cock is rock hard, straining against my jeans, and I think she's purposefully moving against it to cop a feel. I don't fucking care--she can touch me all she wants.

Later on, Chelsea and the gang announce it's time to go. We're all hot and sweaty, and the moment we step outside, the cool air feels good. I follow the group back toward our hotel. Brianne walks beside me. When we're halfway back to The Caribbean, she stops in the middle of the sidewalk.

"Wait! We're going home?"

Everyone laughs, and Chelsea takes her by the arm to make her keep walking. "Yes. It's getting late, and I'm getting *married* tomorrow!"

"Oh, that's right!" Brianne exclaims. "You're going to be Mrs. Carson!"

Everyone laughs at Brianne's drunkenness again. God, she's adorable. I fucking want her.

"No, no," Chelsea says with a giggle. "I'll be Mrs. Willis."

"No more Chelsea McDonald," Brianne says with a sigh, then suddenly turns around and points at me. "But your hotty brother will still carry on the family name!"

I laugh, as does everyone else, but I'm also flattered that Brianne called me a hotty. I wish she weren't so drunk right now. I wish *I* weren't this drunk right now. Those last couple of drinks snuck up on us. I was hoping to go to a strip club tonight and have more fun with Brianne... maybe end up in her room tonight. But that won't happen now.

Brianne blows a kiss at me, then turns around and keeps walking.

When we arrive at The Caribbean, Brianne beelines it for a slot machine. Everyone follows her, and a few others pop money into machines, too. Chelsea sticks by Brianne's side, but I decide to join her and stand on her other side.

Brianne turns her head and looks up at me. "I've had good luck today," she says. "I'm going to win again. Just wait."

I watch as Brianne hits the button, betting the highest amount––$5. After a few losses, she wins $20.

"Woohoo!" She pumps a fist in the air.

"Good job!" Chelsea pats her shoulder.

The next turn she loses, but then she hits a bonus.

"Yes!" Brianne exclaims.

Chelsea and I watch as Brianne rakes up more money. She's having a good luck streak. By the time the bonus play ends, she's up over a hundred dollars. She continues to play, losing some, but then hitting some wins. Carson appears at Chelsea's side, and they announce that they're going to their room.

"Are you guys okay?" Chelsea asks us.

"Yeah, we're good," Brianne says as she continues playing. She turns to look at Chelsea briefly. "Good night! Can't wait for tomorrow!"

Chelsea smiles and gives her a hug. Then she looks back

at me. "Please make sure she gets to her room safely. And--" she drops her voice to a whisper and looks at me sternly-- "be a gentleman. This is my best friend."

Rolling my eyes at her, I reply, "Of course I will. You have nothing to worry about."

Chelsea and Carson leave, and as I look around the casino, I see the rest of our party must've gone to their rooms as well. I look at my watch and see it's almost midnight. It's early. For Vegas, anyway.

The slot machine dings with another win for Brianne, and I see her total is now over $300. Not bad for only putting a fifty in the machine to begin with!

She continues to play, then suddenly cashes out. She retrieves the ticket, then stands and looks at me. "Are you tired?" she asks.

Cocking an eyebrow, I reply, "Not really. Why?"

"Let's cash this out and see what kind of trouble we can get into." Brianne waggles her eyebrows, but she also stumbles toward me. I catch her, and she giggles. "I'm fine, I'm fine."

"You're drunk," I say. "You should keep your money and go upstairs to bed."

Her smile widens. "Now you're talkin'," she says with a wink.

I chuckle and shake my head. I'm not sober myself, but I'm more sober than she is. "As much as I'd like to take you up on that offer, I think we need to go to our own rooms and go to sleep so we're not hungover for Chelsea's wedding tomorrow."

Brianne puts her finger on her chin as if she's thinking. "What offer do you want to take me up on? Going out to have fun, or going upstairs to bed?"

I can't help but find her adorable right now, and it's taking all of my willpower to be the perfect gentleman I promised my sister I would be.

I lean in closer to Brianne and answer in her ear, "Both."

She gasps, and as I look back at her beautiful face, she blushes.

"Come on. I'll walk you to your room," I say, slipping my arm through hers. "Put that winning ticket in your wallet so you can cash out tomorrow."

Brianne follows my directions, then we head toward the elevators. "What floor are you on?" I ask as I press the button to go up.

"Let me look…" Brianne unzips her wristlet wallet and pulls out the key card holder from the hotel, which has her room number written on it. "7069," she says before giggling. "Floor 7, room 69––the *best* room number." She winks, and I chuckle. Then, the elevator doors open.

We get in, and I punch the button for the seventh floor. As the doors close, Brianne takes me by surprise, moving swiftly so my back is against the wall. "You're fucking hot, Corey," she says before crashing her lips to mine in a scorching kiss.

I kiss Brianne with everything I've got. All that pent-up sexual tension that's been building between us all night is released into this kiss. Our tongues lash together as my arms wrap around her waist, pulling her closer. She lets out the sexiest little moan, so I press my hard cock against her lower belly, causing her to let out another moan.

*Fuck, I want her.*

I don't notice the elevator coming to a stop, but there's suddenly a *ding*, followed by the doors sliding open. Brianne steps back with a sexy smirk on her face before stepping off the elevator. I follow her, wanting to make sure she makes it to her room safely. However, after that kiss, I wonder if she'll ask me to stay. Should I, though? I promised my sister I'd be a gentleman. Not only that, but Brianne is also drunk, and I don't want her to regret doing anything with me tonight.

Brianne unlocks her door, then opens it and stops, turning around to face me.

"Wanna come in?"

*Shit.*

It's as if I have a devil on one shoulder telling me to go for it and an angel on the other telling me to be a good boy. I'm conflicted, although I know I need to do the right thing.

"I really want to... but I think we should say good night so we both get a good night's sleep. Tomorrow's Chelsea's wedding after all."

Brianne purses her lips. "Did Chelsea tell you not to hook up with me?"

"What? No," I say, wondering where she's going with this.

Squinting her eyes as if she's trying to decide whether she believes me or not, she says, "Are you really a player like she said you are?"

My eyebrows shoot up. Chelsea told her that? I mean, she's not exactly wrong, but why the hell is my sister telling Brianne that I'm a player?

"Chelsea said that?"

She nods, then shrugs one shoulder. "It's kinda perfect, really, 'cause I've been known to be a player, too. But it's all good." Brianne steps into her room and begins to close the door, leaving it open just enough to see her face. "I'll see you in the morning, Corey."

She blows me a kiss, then closes the door.

Damn. I'm dumbstruck for a moment, trying to process how I feel about what Chelsea said to her. The thing is, *am* I still a player? Is that what my family thinks? When I was in high school, I was exactly how Brianne described me—scrawny, as well as shy. Girls weren't into me at all. Then, I went to college and worked out, and my entire body changed. I became this attractive guy who women fawned over. Going from getting *no* attention to getting *all* the attention from girls, I realized I could date as many as I wanted. I never intentionally hurt anyone, but I also never wanted to be in a committed relationship either. I just wanted to have fun.

And, boy, did I have fun. Up until last year, when I took over Uncle Garret's company and no longer had time to go out as often as I used to. Over the course of this year, many of my friends have started to settle down in serious relationships as well, and I see how happy they are. I don't want my reputation of being a player to precede me.

I head back to the elevator and push the up button again. Sure, I could have a good time with Brianne this weekend, but how will it play out, especially considering she's my sister's best friend? It's not as if I'll never see her again. And maybe I'll *want* to see her again. What if *that* happens?

The elevator arrives, and I push the button for the tenth floor to go to my room. My phone buzzes in my pocket, and I take it out to find a text from *her* again. Seline. I hadn't heard from her since she texted me earlier today, but I guess she's back at it again. I open the text and see that she sent me a selfie. Her hair and makeup are all done up, like she went out with friends or something. There's no text, just the picture. I close the text and slide my phone back in my pocket. If I keep ignoring her, she'll eventually get the hint.

38

I arrive on the tenth floor and walk down the hall toward my room. I think back to how fun it was to go out with Chelsea, Carson, and all their friends tonight. Especially Brianne. Watching the burlesque show with her, then dancing together at the club--I had a fucking hard on all night long. That kiss in the elevator was unfuckingbelievable, too. I'm attracted to Brianne in a way that I haven't felt with anyone else... which is probably due to the crush I had on her growing up. I can't believe I just turned down the chance to have sex with her. We could be down in her room together right now getting it on. I deserve a medal for doing the right thing and saying good night to her instead.

I unlock my door and enter my room. After I set my key and wallet on the dresser, I walk over to the window and look out at the glittering lights on the strip. I find it ironic how Sin City holds so much potential--for having a lot of fun or getting into a lot of trouble. For a while tonight, I thought Brianne and I might get into a little bit of trouble together. The idea of visiting a strip club came up at one point. Maybe that's someplace we'll end up together tomorrow night. Fuck, that'd be hot.

Tomorrow's going to be a long, exciting day. My sister is getting married. I know it's going to be fun, spending time with my family, then partying it up again tomorrow night to celebrate Chelsea and Carson's wedding. I pray to God I'll have another shot with Brianne... although the worries I have about hooking up with my sister's best friend still linger in the back of my mind. Something tells me Brianne may be worth the risk, though.

# Brianne

## FIVE

I t's too early. Why is my alarm going off so early? I open
my eyes just enough to find my phone on the bedside
table, reach for it, and turn it off. I peek at the screen and see
it's already nine o'clock. Shit. It's not really that early. I have
to meet Chelsea and all the girls for brunch at ten thirty, so I
should get up and get ready. I don't exactly feel hungover,
I'm just overly tired. I need coffee ASAP.

Dragging myself out of bed, thoughts of last night come
flooding back. Corey. Holy shit. He turned me down when I
invited him in... I'm not sure what to think about that. We
had a great time together prior to that--no, actually, an
*amazing* time. The flirting, the dancing, *that kiss.* After
kissing in the elevator, I thought for sure Corey would take
me up on my offer, so I'm confused as to why he didn't. Was
he being a gentleman? Is it because I'm his sister's best
friend? Or is he just not that into me?

I guess I'll find out later today when I see him. Hopefully, he doesn't avoid me. Corey was a lot of fun to hang
out with last night, and I'd like to spend more time with

him. Based on how last night ended, though, I have no idea what to expect from him today. The unknown makes me feel a bit anxious, and I wish I didn't have to wait so long to see him again. Chances are, I won't see him until the wedding later this afternoon.

I make a pot of coffee, then get in the shower.

∼

Once I'm dressed and ready, I head down to meet the girls for brunch. The elevator stops on the fifth floor, and to my surprise, Olivia is there.

"Good morning!" She hugs me as she gets on the elevator.

"How are you? Did you sleep well?" I ask as the doors slide closed again.

She nods. "Yeah, pretty good. What about you? You were still gambling when we went to bed."

"I didn't stay up much later than you guys. Corey and I went to our rooms shortly after everyone else."

"Oh," she says. "So... you two looked cozy together. Is something going on there?"

Shrugging, my mind races with whether to tell her what happened last night. I'm not usually one to hide things from my friends, but this situation is different. Plus, nothing *really* happened between us other than a kiss and him turning me down.

"I don't know," I say. "We had fun last night, but nothing happened."

We reach the lobby, and the elevator doors slide open. Olivia and I start walking, not sure exactly where the restaurant is located. Our conversation about Corey ends abruptly as we try to find out where we're meeting everyone. It's just as well... I honestly don't know what to say about what's going on between Corey and me.

Olivia and I find the restaurant and wait just outside the entrance, just as Chelsea had instructed us to do via text this morning.

"Do you know how you're going to do your hair today?" Olivia asks. "I'm not sure what to do with mine."

Now this is a question I can answer. "I was thinking of leaving my hair down and curling it. I think yours would look good that way, too. Maybe even pull a few strands back like this––" I pull some of her hair back to show her what I mean.

"That's actually what I was thinking, too," she says. "I just wanted your expert opinion before making my final decision."

"I think that'll make you look hot, especially with the dress you're wearing. Alex will have a hard on for you all day."

Olivia laughs at my comment. As Chelsea's only bridesmaids, Olivia and I picked out similar dresses in the same light-gold color. Both are mid-length, but hers has a halter top while mine is lower cut.

"It's my wedding day!" Chelsea exclaims, walking toward us with her arms in the air.

"Woohoo!" Olivia and I greet her with hugs as she walks up to us, along with her mom and Carson's mom.

"Have you been waiting long?" she asks.

"No, we just got here," Olivia says.

Just then, Jolene and Sasha walk up and join us, and Chelsea throws her arms in the air once more. "It's my wedding day!" she announces again.

Sasha and Jolene throw their hands up in excitement, too.

"Shall we go in?" Chelsea's mom says, pointing toward the restaurant.

We walk into the Jamaican-themed restaurant. Chelsea's mom tells the hostess we have reservations, and we're seated right away. We look over the menu, and I'm curious to try several of the breakfast choices they have. I've never had Jamaican food before, and it all sounds intriguing, especially the hibiscus mimosas.

"What exactly is the agenda today, Chelsea?" Olivia asks.

"We have hair appointments at the hotel's salon at one o'clock. After that, we'll get dressed and do makeup in my room, and the wedding starts at three."

"Cool. So, we have a little time after breakfast to play a few slots?" I ask, remembering I won more money last night and have a ticket to cash out.

"For sure," Chelsea says with a wink.

"Taylor texted me this morning," Carson's mom pipes in. "She said they'll get here just in time for the wedding."

"Okay, good," Chelsea says with a smile, although I know neither she nor Carson are thrilled about his sister being here. I don't think his parents know about the fallout Carson and Taylor had. Chelsea told me that they *did* tell his parents how Taylor lied about Alex before, simply so there wouldn't be tension since he's now with Olivia. But I don't think his parents know that Carson and Taylor aren't on the best of terms for other reasons.

Our server comes to take our orders. Along with a hibiscus mimosa, I order Jamaican banana fritters with eggs and bacon. My mind drifts to Corey again, and I wonder what he's doing right now. The guys were all meeting up to eat as well, but not until lunch time. I wonder what he's wearing to the wedding. I bet he looks good in a suit. His taut arms in a white button-up shirt would be sexy as hell...

I wonder what things will be like between us today. Will he still flirt with me? Will we hang out again tonight? I fucking hope so! I just don't understand why he rejected me when I invited him into my room last night. The way he kissed me... *ugh!*

I squirm in my seat, hoping to squelch the ache developing between my legs. I want Corey. I want to feel the fire that ignited between us when we kissed last night. I want to explore his body and feel his hands touch every inch of mine. I don't want to leave Vegas not knowing what could've happened between us.

This isn't like me. Usually, if a guy isn't into me I say fuck it and move on. What is it about Corey that I'm so damn attracted to? It's both exhilarating and infuriating. I don't want to chase after a man, but I also don't want to leave Corey alone. The thought of seeing him later excites me. Honestly, I don't remember the last time I felt this way.

Breakfast is delicious. Afterward, we head to the casino and play a few slots. When it's time to head to the salon, I'm up another fifty bucks! This has been a lucky weekend for me!

Maybe my luck will continue tonight with Corey.

"Holy shit. This is it!" Chelsea fans her face, standing in front of Olivia and me looking gorgeous as I've ever seen her before. Her hair is curled with half of it pulled back. Her veil flows down her back, the lace matching the sheer white lace on her wedding dress. She looks amazing, and Carson is going to be beside himself when he sees her.

"You look beautiful," Olivia says. "And this is so exciting!"

Olivia looks dazzling as well. She has taken my advice with her hair, and her makeup turned out perfect as well.

"I think you'll be next," Chelsea says to her. "You'll be standing in a white dress like this before you know it."

Olivia shakes her head. "I don't know. We'll see." She blushes, and I know that's what she wants. She and Alex are madly in love, and I agree with Chelsea––they'll probably get hitched before too long.

Then both of my best friends will be married.

And I'll still be single.

For some reason, that thought seems weird to me. It's not as if I've never considered this before, but I've never had a sense of loneliness when thinking about it. Why is that? It's not as if my friends are going to *leave* me. I mean, Olivia already lives a few hours away, so what difference will it make if she's married, too?

"Are you okay?" Chelsea asks, and when I look up to see who she's talking to, I realize she's asking *me.*

I shake the feeling and smile. "Of course," I say, shoving my thoughts away. "I'm ready to par-tay and celebrate your wedding!"

Suddenly, I get a tingly feeling, and the hair on my arms stand up.

"Hey, Mom," I hear a familiar, deep, *sexy* voice say behind me.

"Corey, you look so handsome," Chelsea's mom says.

My stomach flip flops as I realize Corey's here, standing behind me somewhere.

"Corey!" Chelsea moves past me to go to her brother. "You look great!"

I'm hesitant to turn around. I've thought about him all day, so why am I afraid to see him now? Why am I afraid to see him, *period*? Realization hits that nothing about the way I am with Corey is normal for me, and I'm not quite sure how to feel about that.

I look at Olivia, and she's on her phone, probably texting Alex. That lonely feeling hits me again, and it pisses me off. Why the fuck am I feeling so emotional today? Screw these *feelings*--I'm not afraid of any man, so why should I be afraid to turn around and face Corey now?

*Because he rejected you last night.* The little voice in my head reminds me.

Fuck this. This isn't me.

Taking a deep breath, I turn around with a smile on my face, ready to have a good time and enjoy my best friend's wedding--regardless of how her brother feels about me.

But I don't see him right away. Chelsea is standing in front of Corey as she explains how he'll walk their mom down the aisle.

I take a few steps closer, and when he comes into my view, he turns to look at me.

Jesus. His lips slowly curl up in a smile, and his entire face seems to light up. "Hey, Brianne." My name rolls off his tongue like honey, and I feel frozen in my tracks.

"Hey," I manage to say in return as my heart pounds in my chest. Nervously, I smooth my hair with my hands.

"You look nice," he adds, and suddenly, I feel as if we're the only two people in the room.

I clear my throat. "So do you."

We hold eye contact for a moment, and although we're

standing several feet away from each other, I can feel the electricity pulsing between us. Is my attraction to Corey that strong?

"Honey, you didn't get a boutonniere?" their mom asks, suddenly realizing Corey isn't wearing one.

"Oh, I know we ordered him one," Chelsea says in a panic.

Corey drags his eyes from me and looks at his mom. "I didn't know I was supposed to wear one."

Suddenly, that's the only thing that matters—where Corey's boutonniere could possibly be. The hotel's wedding planner rushes over and promises to track it down.

"You like him, don't you?" Olivia whispers in my ear.

I turn to look at her, surprised by her question. "Um..."

She smiles. "It's okay. Your secret's safe with me."

Olivia winks, then walks over to Chelsea to assure her that Corey's missing boutonniere isn't the end of the world. Meanwhile, I'm dumbfounded that Olivia picked up on my feelings. Am I that obvious? I need to stop whatever I'm doing and act natural so other people don't catch on. I decide to excuse myself to use the restroom.

Within a few minutes, the wedding planner returns with Corey's boutonniere and pins the red rose onto his shirt. "It's time to go," she announces.

I grab the bouquet I'm carrying, then follow everyone out of the hotel suite. Chelsea and Carson splurged for their wedding, and we used their room to get ready in while the guys all got ready in Carson's parents' room on another floor.

We follow the wedding planner down the elevator, through the hotel, and out to the beach area. She instructs us where to stand under a large tent that's hidden from the ceremony's view. Once we walk out of the tent, we'll walk down the aisle to the altar.

Corey and his mom are the first to walk out. Shortly after they leave, she tells Olivia to go. Butterflies stir in my belly as I wait my turn to go. Why do I have this nervous feeling? *I'm* not the one getting married! But before I can analyze my feelings for the millionth time today, the wedding planner tells me to go.

Straightening my posture and plastering a smile on my face, I walk with as much confidence I can muster and head down the aisle.

It's a gorgeous day with the sun shining in a clear blue sky. It looks as though we're on a beach somewhere, not at a hotel in Vegas. There are more people than I expect to see sitting at the wedding. I know both Chelsea and Carson had other relatives come to town for the wedding, but since they weren't involved in any of the pre-wedding activities, I hadn't met them. I see Alex, Sasha, and Jolene. Then, on the opposite side of the aisle, I notice Taylor and her husband, who seem more smug than happy to be here. *Assholes.*

And then I see Corey, next to his mom, watching me with the sexiest smile on his face. His gaze makes me feel more empowered––not nervous like before, but more like I want to show off for him. I want him to notice me, find me attractive, to *want* me as much as I want him.

*This* is more like me. I want to flirt with Corey and make myself utterly irresistible to him.

I make my way to the altar and stand next to Olivia. Carson, Aaron, and Bryan are standing on the other side with the woman who is officiating the wedding in the middle. I look in Corey's direction again, and he smirks at me just as the wedding march begins.

Everyone turns their attention toward Chelsea and her dad, who are walking down the aisle. She looks absolutely radiant. I look at Carson to see his reaction to his beautiful bride. He wipes his eye, and I know he's overwhelmed with his love for her. The two of them have so much love for one another, I know he's the right man for her. None of Chelsea's other boyfriends ever cared for her in the same way Carson does. If there is such a thing as soul mates, I'd say Carson and Chelsea definitely are.

Chelsea and her dad stop in front of the altar, and the officiant asks, "Who gives this woman to this man?"

"Her mother and I do," her dad replies before taking his seat next to his wife.

What a weird tradition that is. I'm surprised people still "give away" their daughters when they get married. It's the twenty-first century after all, not the 1800s. I guess some traditions are hard to break.

As the ceremony goes on, I can't help but be overcome with emotion again. Is my period going to start soon or something? I'm *never* this emotional, even at weddings. I don't know why, but I'm sensitive today. I refuse to believe it has to do with Corey. But when I look over at him, and his head turns toward me at the same time, I know there's something special about him. The connection we have is too damn strong to deny it.

I turn my attention back toward Chelsea and Carson and keep it there for the rest of the ceremony. No matter how many times I feel drawn to look at Corey, I force myself not to. Maybe playing a little hard to get will be good.

"You may now kiss the bride!" Carson and Chelsea kiss each other sweetly as everyone claps and cheers for them.

Then, they turn and head back up the aisle, followed by Aaron and me, then Bryan and Olivia.

I don't make eye contact with Corey as I walk, either. But I make sure I'm smiling and happy the entire time.

We stop at the same tent we started at, and the wedding planner tells us that the reception area will be ready in an hour, after pictures. I had forgotten about the photos, and I look at Chelsea and ask what she wants us to do.

"Let's take some photos with everyone first," she says, "And then you can all go hang out for a bit while we do the rest of the pictures of just us."

"Sounds like a plan," I reply as we head out to the photo spot.

Although Corey is present for the photos, I don't interact with him at all. The photographer instructs us all where to stand and what to do for the photos, and once we're done, we're excused to go.

"Meet us at the reception in thirty minutes!" Chelsea calls out so everyone hears.

Olivia and Alex walk off together, seemingly trying to avoid Taylor and her husband. I don't blame them. So far, Taylor seems pretentious and annoying. She and Carson are nothing alike.

"Hey," Corey says, suddenly standing right in front of me.

"Oh, hey," I reply, trying to sound casual when in reality my heart rate just increased ten-fold.

"Want to grab a drink?" he asks.

Relief that he wants to spend time with me again floods my veins, and I crack a smile. "That sounds like a great idea."

Corey bends his elbow out toward me so I can slip my arm through his. "Come on," he says, and I can't resist.

As I slip my arm through his, he whispers in my ear, "You look fucking gorgeous."

My heart skips a beat as my brain suddenly turns to mush.

"Thank you," I manage to say, hoping he can't tell how flustered I am. "You look fucking great yourself."

We walk together, and I hope we find a bar soon. I need to calm these nerves of mine.

# *Corey*

## SIX

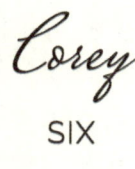

Now that I have Brianne by my side, I can relax. I woke up nervous this morning, worried she wouldn't want to have anything to do with me today. Although we had a fun time together last night, I had wondered if she felt rejected by me when I refused her invitation to go in her room. Then, when I finally got a chance to see her today, I couldn't read her. She wasn't as friendly with me as she was last night. She almost seemed to be avoiding me.

Even during the wedding ceremony, she wouldn't look in my direction. A couple of times we made eye contact, but she quickly looked away. Seeing her, looking as beautiful as she is and knowing how her soft lips feel against mine... I've been dying to touch her again. As soon as she slips her arm through mine, I feel more at ease than I've felt all day.

We don't have to walk far before we arrive at one of the many bars The Caribbean has to offer. "Want to sit at the bar or at one of the tables?" I ask her.

"A table would be more comfortable in this dress and

heals," she replies, and I take the opportunity to look at her beautiful body up and down.

"God, you're sexy." I want to make sure she's aware just how attracted I am to her.

She giggles as we sit. "Thank you. So are you."

I smile. Hearing her say she thinks I'm sexy makes me feel good. I don't want to dwell on how she feels about me after last night, and I want to know if she was upset with me for leaving, so I dive right in. "So, about last night..."

She cocks an eyebrow. "What about last night?"

The server arrives at our table, and we both turn to look at him. He tells us about a few specials they have, and then we both place our order. I ask for a Jack and Coke, and she asks for a margarita on the rocks, no salt.

"So, it's tequila today?" I say once our server walks away.

She nods. "Yep. I like variety."

"Is that right?" I ask. "You like mixing it up?"

"Of course. Life would be dull otherwise."

I lean my elbows on the table and move a bit closer to her. "I like variety as well, but once I find something I like, I tend to stick with it."

"Really?" Brianne looks at me, pursing her lips, as if she's considering what I said. "And what do you like?"

I just look at her for a beat before answering her question truthfully. "I like you, Brianne."

Her mouth drops open, and I think I've surprised her.

"So, like I was saying, about last night... I hope you're not mad at me for leaving."

She breaks eye contact with me and looks down for a second before looking back at me. "It's totally fine. I'm not mad."

"Are you sure? Because I've been worried about it ever since I walked away from you last night."

"I'm sure, Corey. I was really drunk... so it was the right thing for you to do."

"Oh," I say, unsure of what she means by that exactly.

She leans in a bit closer and places her hand on my arm. "But for the record, I wasn't so drunk that I didn't know what I was doing."

My smile spreads slowly, understanding exactly what she means. She wanted me last night. Hopefully, she still wants me today.

Our server returns with our drinks, and we both sit back in our chairs.

God, I hope everything goes well with Brianne tonight.

"Carson and I would like to thank our parents for everything they've done to help us with this day. We are forever grateful for all your help and generosity." Chelsea gives her toast as she and Carson stand next to the elegant white two-tier cake with a bride and groom standing on top. "We'd also like to thank the rest of our family members for coming, and of course, our friends who traveled here for this special day. We love you all!"

Everyone claps as they hold their champagne flutes up, toasting Chelsea and Carson. Then we all take a sip of the champagne. I look at Brianne, standing next to the cake table, along with Olivia. The two of them had given a nice joint speech prior to Chelsea's, talking about how happy they are for their best friend, bringing a tear to Chelsea's eye. Aaron and Bryan had also given a speech. Now the speeches seem to be over, and Chelsea and Carson are ready to cut the cake.

I always like to predict how this part of the reception will go at weddings. Either the couple can be sweet and feed each other a piece of cake neatly without getting messy, or they'll slam the cake into each other's faces, which is always entertaining to watch.

Carson and Chelsea go the sweet route. They each carefully feed a piece of cake to the other, being careful not to make a mess. Everyone sighs in unison at how nice they are. I kind of wish they'd been a bit more exciting.

Once they're done, everyone gets cake and heads back to the tables to sit and eat. The reception is in a small room, just large enough for the thirty or so people who came to the wedding. A few of my cousins, as well as my aunt and uncle flew down for the wedding, and it's been nice catching up with them today. It's been a pretty typical wedding reception with dinner, drinks, and now cake. They didn't hire a DJ, though, so there won't be a lot of dancing; however, Chelsea and Carson did bring a portable speaker so they can have their first dance as a married couple, and also do the dad/daughter and mother/son dance. I have a feeling they'll do that as soon as everyone is finished eating cake.

Luckily, Brianne and I are able to sit next to each other. We end up sitting at the same table as Olivia, Alex, Chelsea, and Carson, so it's been a fun evening. And, our fun evening won't end when this reception is over. Chelsea and Carson want everyone to go out again tonight, so we have that to look forward to. I'm hoping things will happen with Brianne, and by the way things are going, I'd say there's a good chance for that.

"This cake is delicious!" Brianne closes her eyes as she

savors the delicious cake in her mouth. It's an innocent gesture, but it makes my cock twitch. She's sexy even when she doesn't intend to be.

"Mmmm, this *is* good," Olivia agrees as she takes another bite.

Watching Olivia eat does nothing for me. I'm only attracted to Brianne.

"Tonight should be fun," Alex says. "I wonder where we'll end up going?"

"I don't know, but I'm sure we'll have fun wherever we end up," I reply.

Chelsea and Carson are mingling with other guests, so it's just the four of us at the table.

"I hope we go dancing again," Brianne says before taking another bite.

"I do, too. That was fun last night." *And, I want the chance to hold your beautiful body close to mine while we dance again.*

"You don't think Taylor and Wayne will go out with us, do you?" Alex asks, looking nervous at the thought.

Olivia puts her hand on his knee and looks him square in the eye. "If they do go, we'll just keep our distance. Just like we've managed to do all day."

I can't imagine being at a wedding with an ex who told lies about me. Talk about awkward. Luckily, Alex hasn't had any issues so far today. Hopefully, that continues.

"Man, I wish we could stay here another day or two. I don't want to go home to the rainy Oregon weather," Olivia says, changing the subject.

"That would be fun," Brianne agrees with her.

The thought of staying another night or two with Brianne sounds amazing. I'd love to have more time with her, especially without all the wedding festivities dictating our schedule. There's tons of things to do in Vegas, and it would be fun to experience some of them with her.

Realization hits that I don't have much on my schedule for Monday. I purposely kept my schedule open knowing I might need an extra day to recover from Vegas. Olivia's idea is intriguing, and I wonder if I'd be able to change my flight and hotel reservation to stay another day. I wonder if Brianne would be able to stay another day, too? I'll keep this idea in mind and maybe bring it up again later, depending on how tonight goes.

Suddenly, we hear the clanking of someone tapping against a wine glass. We turn our attention and see my dad standing near the cake table again, ready to make another speech.

"Ladies and gentlemen, we have the music ready for Chelsea and Carson to have their first dance as husband and wife."

Everyone cheers, and Chelsea and Carson get ready to dance. The music starts, and the two of them begin slow dancing together.

"Aw, I love this song," Olivia says, resting her head on Alex's shoulder.

I look at Brianne, watching Chelsea and Carson. I can't get over how beautiful she is. I was always attracted to her when we were younger, so it's surreal for me to be sitting next to Brianne now. Thirteen-year-old me would find it hard to believe this... but he'd also be *very* happy.

I finish eating my cake as we all watch Chelsea and Carson. Once the song ends, another song starts, and Chelsea grabs our dad's hand while Carson takes his mom's to dance. Everyone watches as they dance together, and halfway through the song, Carson's dad cuts in to dance with Chelsea, while Mom cuts in to dance with Carson. It's a sweet moment, and everyone else watching seems to agree.

Once the song ends, another slow one starts, and Carson announces, "We'd like everyone to come up and dance to this one!"

All of the couples in the room make their way to the dance floor, including Olivia and

Alex, leaving Brianne and me alone at the table. Brianne takes the last bite of her piece of cake, and I decide I can't let this opportunity slip by.

"Would you like to dance?" I ask her.

Brianne looks at me, wide eyed. She swallows the food in her mouth. "In front of your family?"

I chuckle. "Yeah. Who cares?"

She shrugs, then wipes her mouth with a napkin. "I don't know. Won't they get the wrong idea or ask you annoying questions?"

I shrug, then stand, putting my hand out for her to take. "I don't care what they think. Besides, it's just a dance. We're the only ones not dancing... aside from my cousins who are brother and sister."

Brianne smiles, then takes my hand and stands. "Let's do this."

We join everyone else dancing. I put one hand on Brianne's hip and hold her hand in my other. I go the traditional route dancing with her in front of my family. It's definitely not as intimate as how we danced at the club last night, but it's obviously more appropriate.

Dancing this way, though, makes it possible to look into Brianne's eyes as we move together, and I quickly realize that this is a different kind of intimate. My heart pounds in my chest as I look into her eyes, admiring how beautiful she looks, feeling as if I'm the luckiest man in the room to be dancing with her. The moment is over far too soon when she breaks our eye contact and looks away. It doesn't bother me, though. It feels incredible to hold her in my arms, and if I have my way, we'll have the chance to get closer tonight.

As we continue dancing, I look around at all of the couples dancing. My parents, who've been married for thirty years now, look happy as ever. I've only been in love once in my life, back when I was a sophomore in college. I started seeing this girl named Penny, and I was exclusive with her for about a month––which, for me, was a long time. We spent nearly every moment together during that time, and when she told me she was falling in love with me, I told her the same. That's the closest I've ever come to being in love, and while it didn't end well (she actually cheated on me), I *do* know what it feels like to be in love.

At least, I think I do. I'm not sure if my "love" for Penny was really love, or just a strong infatuation. The fact that my only experience in that department lasted only a month suddenly makes me wonder if there's something wrong with me. I'd like to find a love like the one my parents have, and one day have a family of my own. Although I've never been in a long-term relationship, I've always pictured myself married with kids one day––in the future. But how far into the future? I'm already twenty-five. Sure, I'm still young, but I also feel ready to at least have a *real,* committed relationship. What's holding me back?

My job, for one. I'm always busy. This weekend is an anomaly and a much-needed vacation. I turned my work phone off and left it in my suitcase so I wouldn't be distracted. But even though work *does* keep me busy, I also know part of the reason is because I do it to myself. The business is doing so well, I can afford to hire another employee to take some of the pressure off myself. It's something I've been thinking about for a couple of months now, but I've put it off for one reason and one reason only––to save money. However, I think it may be worth it now. Especially if it'll give me more free time for dating.

Maybe I can convince Brianne to go out with me once we're back home.

Maybe I'm getting ahead of myself.

Brianne turns her head to look at me again, but the song ends. She steps away from me, but I hold onto her hand, which takes her by surprise.

"Thanks for dancing with me," I say, taking a step closer to her again.

She smiles shyly, which is unlike Brianne. She's never shy.

I lean in closer and whisper in her ear, "I want another dance later."

I look back at her, and her shyness is replaced with a more confident smile. "We'll see about that," she says with a wink, then drops her hand from mine and walks away.

*Damn.* If she's playing hard to get, it's definitely working like a charm.

# *Brianne*

## SEVEN

"Let's go change our clothes and meet back down here in thirty minutes."

Everyone agrees to Chelsea's suggestion, then heads toward the elevators. The wedding reception is officially over, but Chelsea and Carson have invited us all to go out and celebrate more. Bryan suggests another dance club he's familiar with that sounds like a lot of fun, so those of us who went out last night, as well as Carson's sister and her husband, and a few of their cousins who are close to us in age, agree to go out.

We pile into an elevator and head up to our rooms. Corey has been by my side all night, and now that we're in close quarters in the elevator, my back is pressed to his front, and his hand is on my hip. I don't want to move. I don't want to lose his touch. But the elevator stops on the seventh floor, and I have to get off.

"See you guys soon," I say as I step off the elevator. Before the doors slide shut, I catch Corey's eye and give him a wink.

I hope to have as much fun, if not more, than I had with Corey last night. No, that's not true. I want to have *a lot* more fun than we had last night. After spending all evening together at the wedding, I have one goal tonight and one goal only––to wind up in bed with Corey.

I want him. My attraction to Corey is stronger than anything I've ever experienced, and the sexual tension between us has built up to the point that it's about to explode. I don't want to hold back any longer. Why should I be afraid of hooking up with Corey? So, he's my best friend's brother... the more I think about it, the more I see that as a good thing. What if things actually work out with Corey and go beyond just hooking up in Vegas? It's my best friend's brother––how cool is that? And if we don't work out––I know my friendship with Chelsea won't waver. Our friendship is solid and always will be. I know that for a fact.

After I change out of my bridesmaid's dress and put on the form-fitting, off-the-shoulder, mini black dress I brought with me, as well as touch up my hair and makeup, I head back down to the lobby to meet everyone. Corey is one of the last to arrive, and he looks hot as hell in a taut black t-shirt and gray pants that show off the dips and curves of his muscles. He's fit and in good shape, and I yearn to explore his body tonight.

We leave the hotel and walk to the one next door, which has the popular night club inside. This time, we don't get the royal treatment and have to wait in a line, but Bryan and Sasha assure us it's worth the wait. Corey stands by my side, and although we're not touching, I still feel a magnetic pull toward him.

"How long have you two been together?" Taylor asks as we wait in line. She and her husband are standing behind us, far from Olivia and Alex who are a little further ahead of us in line. Alex has tried to stay away from Taylor ever since they arrived, and so far, he's been successful.

Confused by Taylor's question, I look to my side to see who she might be talking to.

"I was asking you," she says to me. "Aren't you and him a couple?" Taylor points at

Corey, which grabs his attention as well.

Shaking my head, I tell her, "No, no. We're not a couple."

Her eyebrows knit inward. "You're not? I thought for sure you were."

I look at Corey, and he smiles. "I've known Brianne practically my whole life, but we're not really together."

That one little word--*really*--hangs in the air as Taylor responds to him, but I'm not paying attention. We're not *really* together... what did he mean by that, exactly? Of course, we're not a couple, so we're not together. But *really* could mean a couple of things. Does he mean that we're just having fun while we're in Vegas, but we're not *really ever* going to be a couple? Or, did he mean it to say we're just not *really* an *official* couple? I'm curious what Corey's end game is for us. Is he just looking for a good time while we're in Sin City, or could he possibly want more?

Taylor laughs. I have no idea what was said between her and Corey that was funny, though, since I'm distracted with my thoughts. "Well, if my opinion's worth anything, I thought you two were definitely an item. You make a very attractive couple."

"Thanks. That's nice of you," Corey says.

I force a smile but don't say anything else. The line

moves, so we move forward, closer to the door. There are only three couples ahead of us now, so hopefully, we'll get in soon.

Taylor and her husband, who's several years older than the rest of us, are like the black sheep of our group and have no shame in showing PDA. He suddenly snakes his hand around her, palming her ass, as they proceed to kiss--passionately--in front of us all. I'm sure her brother is thrilled to see it, let alone her ex, Alex. I usually have no problem with people being affectionate in front of me, but there's something about the two of them that I can't stand. I look over and notice that Olivia and Alex are standing next to Chelsea and Carson, and all four of them look disgusted at the scene playing out in front of us.

Gross.

I turn around, and to my surprise, Corey puts his arm around me. "She has a point," he

says in my ear.

I turn my head to look at him, confused by what he means. "What?"

He smirks, then leans in close again so only I can hear him say, "We make an attractive couple."

His breath sends a tingle down my neck, and I can't help but feel turned on by it.

I smirk back at him. "Yeah, we do," I say, cocking an eyebrow.

The line moves forward again as the three couples in front of our group are let into the club. Hopefully, it'll be our turn soon.

Corey's arm stays where it is around my waist as he stands close to me. "You look so fucking sexy in this dress," he whispers in my ear. "I like how short it is."

"Is that right?" I say quietly. My stomach flutters as the tension between us continues to build.

"Mmmhmm." He turns to whisper in my ear again, but this time his tongue glides along the edge of it, causing me to squirm. I feel the wetness pooling at my core, and I wish I had chosen *not* to wear any panties tonight. "I want to take you to a dark corner of this club."

"Oh?" My voice is barely a whisper.

"I want you, Brianne." Hearing his words and my name rolling off his tongue sends my heart into my throat, and I'm speechless. Corey and I are on the same page in terms of where we want things to go tonight, and the realization of that is exhilarating.

The line moves forward, and we finally make our way inside the dance club. The bass from the music pounds my chest, and the different-colored lights make it feel as if we're entering another world––one full of debauchery and satisfaction. We follow everyone else in our group to the bar, which is in the center of the main floor, surrounded by the dance floor. I look up and see a second-story dance floor that hangs over half of the main floor, and the DJ is also located on the second story on a platform across from the dance floor.

As we wait at the bar to order drinks, Corey keeps his hand around my waist. The bar is crowded, and I'm not even sure if anyone else in our party notices how close the two of us are standing to each other. Corey leans in close so I can hear him over the music. "I can't keep my hands off you. You're so fucking sexy."

His words have a direct line to my libido, and I want Corey more than I've wanted him all weekend. How can we sneak out of here together? As much as I want to have fun and celebrate my best friend's wedding, I'm also dying to get close and personal with her brother... and I'm honestly not sure how long I can wait before I combust.

I look at Corey and lick my lips seductively, then brush my thumb against his lip. His eyes dance with anticipation as everything around us seems to disappear. I forget about everyone around us and lean closer so I can speak in his ear. "I think *you're* fucking sexy, and I want your hands all over my body while I explore yours."

Corey's hand grips my hip, and I know I'm having an effect on him. I look at his face again, and the heated passion in his eyes turns me on even more.

"Brianne, what do you want?" Chelsea's voice interrupts our moment, and I turn to look at my friend, who's gotten the bartender's attention.

"Oh, um, I guess a margarita," I say over the loud music.

Chelsea smiles and nods her head in acknowledgement, and then her eyes catch Corey's arm around my waist. She cocks an eyebrow and looks at me a beat longer before turning back around toward the bartender.

I wonder what she's thinking and if she'll say anything to me about getting so close to her brother.

Corey's breath is on my neck again. "I don't care what my sister thinks. You're fucking mine tonight."

I squirm, and a smile spreads across my face. Corey and I are on the same page, and I can't wait to see how things progress between us.

Chelsea hands me a margarita, grabbing my attention again.

"Thanks!" I tell her.

Chelsea leads the way toward the dance floor, taking my hand and pulling me with her. I look back at Corey, who's still waiting to order a drink at the bar, along with Carson, Alex, and the other guys in our group. I shrug at him as Chelsea drags me with her, and I wonder if she's upset about how close her brother and I were standing together.

Once all of us girls are out on the dance floor, we dance together. Chelsea doesn't say anything at first, but after a while, she leans in closer to me. "What's up with you and Corey?"

Trying to act nonchalant, I reply, "I don't know. We're just having fun."

Chelsea looks at me as if she's contemplating what I said. "Just be careful. That's my little brother, you know." She winks, then smiles, and I know she's not mad about Corey and me. I've got a green light.

*Thank God.*

Suddenly, I feel a hand wrap around my waist, then a body pressing against me, dancing in sync to the music. I know immediately that it's Corey--my entire body is in tune with his. Carson and Alex dance with Chelsea and Olivia as well, and I turn around to face Corey, setting my hand on his hip.

We continue dancing and drinking, although I don't need to drink to feel drunk. I already feel intoxicated just from being so close to him. Everyone's having a great time dancing together, but then Corey takes my hand, pulling me away from the group.

I follow him as he leads me across the dance floor, and what he told me earlier replays in my mind--something about wanting to make me come to a dark corner. He takes my almost-empty glass from me and sets it on a table we pass by, along with the glass from his drink.

Corey pulls me to a spot against a wall that's not exactly

secluded, but it's hidden from plain sight. Although we're just feet away from the dance floor, no one's paying attention to us, and the lack of light makes it difficult for people to see us. I can barely make out Corey's face directly in front of me.

"Do you know how hard I've been all night?" he says, pressing his body against mine. My back is against the wall. "Looking at you, all dressed up, looking as gorgeous as you've been all day long."

I gasp as his hand grips my ass, pulling my body closer. His hard cock presses against my belly, and my mouth goes dry. I look at him, but it's too dark to make out all his features. Behind him, I see people dancing on the dance floor, the bright lights moving all around, but narrowly avoiding us here in this corner.

"And I love this dress you're wearing," he continues as his hand drops lower, skimming the hem of my dress against my thigh. "You look amazing--" he kisses my neck-- "sexy--" another kiss-- "and I want you more than you'll ever know." His hand inches up my inner thigh as he peppers kisses along my neck, working his way lower toward my chest.

My head falls back against the wall, and I surrender myself to Corey. His touch excites me, makes me feel wanton, and I don't want him to stop. His hand reaches my panties, and he runs his finger along the front of the silky material. I squirm, his finger just missing my clit. I can feel how wet I am, and I want him to relieve the pressure building inside. I want him to make me come.

Corey's knee gently nudges my leg, so I spread them apart a little further to grant him access. Just as his lips land on mine, kissing me senselessly, he pulls my panties aside, and I feel his fingers against my pussy. I moan into his mouth and buck my hips toward him.

"You like that?" he asks. He rubs his fingers along my lips, then presses against my clit, sending a delicious jolt through my body. "I'm gonna make you come so hard."

His words spur me on, adding to the pleasure he's giving me. He kisses me again, then makes his way down my neck to my chest again, only this time, he doesn't stop. With his free hand, he pulls the top of my dress down, exposing my breast, then swiftly covering my nipple with his mouth.

I moan again as the pleasure continues to build. Corey knows how to drive me wild. I forget that we're in a crowded dance club with people only a few feet away from us. But we're hidden here in the dark, so no one seems to notice. Still, the thought of someone watching us is thrilling—knowing that we could be discovered any moment makes things more exciting.

Corey continues rubbing my clit in circles, and I feel the buildup of my impending orgasm. The flashing lights and people dancing in the near distance fade away, but the pounding bass of the music still pounds in my chest. Closing my eyes, I allow myself to just feel—Corey's mouth on my breast, his fingers pleasuring me, mixed with the vibrations of the music and the possibility of getting caught—and I come, calling Corey's name out as I do.

Suddenly, Corey's mouth covers mine as he kisses me again, and his fingers slow their movements, eventually stopping altogether. My eyes flutter open, and he pulls back. His face is still a shadow, and I wish I could see the expression on his face.

He pulls my dress back up to cover my breast, and I

straighten my posture, smoothing my dress with my hands. I clear my throat, then say, "Thank you."

"Did you like that?" he asks.

I nod, but then realize he may not be able to see me. "Yes, I did. That was amazing, actually."

Corey moves closer to me again to speak in my ear. His breath tickles my neck, and his deep voice makes me weak in the knees. "I want to take you back to the hotel and make you come on my cock."

The muscles in my belly clench. "I want that, too," I say, hoping we'll sneak out of here soon so we can go and do just that.

Corey takes my hand, and we walk back out to the dance floor. We find Chelsea, Carson, Olivia, and Alex and join them dancing. When Olivia and Chelsea see us, they smile wide, seemingly happy to see us.

Chelsea leans in close to talk. "Where were you?"

Shoot. What should I say? I can't exactly tell her the truth.

"Just exploring the club," I say, hoping she'll believe me.

"Did you see what happened?" Olivia asks, and I wonder what she means.

"Carson and Taylor got in an argument, and Taylor and Wayne ended up leaving," Chelsea explains, "It caused a bit of a commotion. You didn't see it?"

Shaking my head, I wonder what happened exactly.

"Carson feels kind of bad, but they were being ridiculous. They were dancing right next to Olivia and Alex as if they were trying to show off or something. It was weird and uncomfortable. Carson asked them to stop, and they ignored him, so he blew up," Chelsea says. "I'm surprised you missed it. Where were you guys?"

"I don't know," I lie, waving my hand toward the corner we were in. "Over there somewhere."

Olivia and Chelsea both eye me, and they look as though they're trying to decide if I'm telling the truth.

"What?" I say, putting both of my hands out in confusion.

My friends drop the inquisition, and we continue dancing with our guys by our sides. As much as I want to go back to the hotel with Corey, I also can't abandon Chelsea on her big day. Luckily, I get the feeling Corey feels the same way because he doesn't even try to sneak us out of the club.

We continue dancing, having a fantastic time with everyone, but I'm craving to be alone with Corey. We dance close to each other, enjoying each other's touch as we move to the music. Finally, he says in my ear, "Let's get out of here. I can't wait much longer."

Nodding, a chill runs through my body. Excited is an understatement--I'm dying to get back to the hotel and have sex with Corey.

He moves past me and says something to his sister, although I can't hear what he says. Then, he says goodbye to Carson while Chelsea turns her attention to me. She wraps her arms around me in a hug. "Be careful," she says. "And have fun."

I give Olivia a hug as well, then say goodbye to the others in our party. Then, Corey and I leave the club and make a beeline to get back to The Caribbean.

# Corey

## EIGHT

I t feels as if I'm walking in sand. Why is it taking so long to get back to our hotel? I know I'm excited to be with Brianne, but I didn't think it would be this difficult to get there. The sidewalk is busy with people. It's Saturday night, so a lot of people are out. Once we finally get to The Caribbean and make our way through the lobby to the elevators, it takes forever for an elevator to come. Eventually, one arrives, and we get on.

"Your room or mine?" I ask Brianne before pushing the floor button.

"Mine, if you don't mind," she says, so I press the number seven.

"I don't mind at all," I tell her as the doors close. "I could care less where we go."

"Is that right?" she says, cocking an eyebrow.

I stalk toward her until her back is pressed against the wall. "Yeah. I don't give a fuck whose room we're in. I just want to be balls deep inside you as soon as fucking possible." I kiss her--hard--until the elevator stops and the doors slide open. Taking her hand, we make our way down the hall to her room.

Quickly, she unlocks her door, then we hurry into the room. She sets her wristlet on the dresser, and I do the same with my wallet. We both kick our shoes off, and then we get right to it, wrapping our arms around each other and kissing each other senseless. Brianne's fingers fumble with the buttons of my shirt, then tears it off me, letting it fall to the floor. I moan in her mouth as she touches my bare chest, running her hands up to my shoulders, down my arms, then to the waistband of my pants.

Our tongues lash together, and I hold the sides of her head. She makes quick work of my pants, letting them fall to the floor, and then I nearly combust when her hand cups my dick.

"Fuck, I want you," I say, then crash my lips to hers again.

I lower my hands to her back and find the zipper of her dress. I unzip it, then pull her dress down, leaving her just in her underwear––a sexy black, silky pair. Her breasts are perky, begging to be touched. I step out of my pants and take the opportunity to admire how beautiful Brianne is. She's drop-dead gorgeous, and I can't believe I'm lucky enough to be with her right now.

We make our way to the bed, and Brianne lies down with one knee up. She looks at me as one of her hands lazily fondles her breast. It's the sexiest sight I've seen in a long time––maybe ever. I watch her for a moment, then pull my boxer briefs off and grip my cock. Brianne's other hand finds her other breast, and I watch as she pleasures herself in front of me. Slowly, I stroke myself.

"God, you're fucking sexy," I say as I step closer to the bed.

She doesn't say anything, she just closes her eyes and gasps as her fingers continue to toy with her taut nipples. I want to suck one in my mouth and pleasure her myself, so I crawl over the top of her and do just that.

"Mmmm... Corey," she gasps as my tongue replaces one of her hands, flicking her nipple back and forth. "That feels good."

My hand replaces her other hand, and I move one knee between her legs, right up against her pussy. At the contact, she rubs herself against me, and I can feel her wetness through the silky material of her panties. *Goddamn--* Brianne has to be the sexiest woman I've ever been with.

"I want you," she says, grinding her pussy against my knee. "I want to feel that dick of yours."

*Jesus Christ.* Her words make me want her more, which I didn't think was possible. I thought I had reached the hilt of how much I wanted Brianne, but apparently, I was wrong. Not only am I physically attracted to her, but she's also bold. If she wants something, she asks for it, including in the bedroom. It's a complete turn on for me, and I'm more than willing to show her just how bold I can be in bed, too.

"Do you want me to fuck you now?" I ask, nipping her nipple gently, causing her to gasp in pleasure. "Do you want me to make you come again?"

My knee is soaked, and I'm dying to strip her out of her panties and taste her, so I do. Moving swiftly, I get off the bed, take her underwear off, then crawl back on the bed, settling between her legs. I look at her bare pussy, glistening with her juices, and drag my finger along it first before diving in with my tongue.

"Yes!" Brianne's back bows off the bed as I lick her up and down, all around. She's so responsive to everything I do to her, which turns me on even more. Not only that, but she also tastes so fucking sweet, I don't think I can ever get enough of her. "Right there," she says, her voice barely a whisper.

I insert a finger and focus my tongue on her clit. Brianne moves against my mouth, and it doesn't take long before I feel her muscles clench around my finger, and she calls out in ecstasy. As she recovers, I take the opportunity to retrieve a condom from my wallet, unwrap it, and slide it onto my cock.

"I want you," she says, leaning up on her elbows to look at me. "I've never come so fast in my life, and I want to know what that dick of yours can do."

*Fuck.* "Oh, yeah?" Holding my shaft in my hand, I stroke it a couple of times. "You want to come on my cock?"

She nods and licks her lips in the most seductive way. "Yes, please. Fuck me, Corey."

Her words send a thrill through my body, and I don't hesitate. Crawling back over her, I align myself at her entrance and slide all the way in. She moans in pleasure, and I can't help but moan as well. She feels so silky, so wet, so tight––so perfect.

We move together slowly at first, then I pick up the pace. I fuck her as deep as I can from this missionary position, but I want to get deeper. Quickly, I pull out of her, and for a split second, I see the confusion on her face, until I grip her legs and flip her over to her stomach. She gasps at the sudden move, and then I grip her hips, pulling them up off the bed so she's on her knees and her ass is in the air.

"Oh!" She turns her head to look back at me. "Are you gonna spank me?"

Smiling at her question, I promptly smack her ass, causing her to squeal and laugh. "Have I been naughty?" she asks, her voice like honey.

I get myself into position and spank her again. "You're so fucking naughty, I'm going to have to fuck you harder as punishment."

"That doesn't sound like a punishment. I like being fucked hard."

My cock twitches. Brianne is spicier than I expected, and I love it. I smack her ass one more time before sliding my dick back inside her, causing both of us to moan in pleasure. I slide in deeper from this position, which works out better for both of us. I can tell she's close to coming again, so I reach my hand around to rub her clit, and once I do, it doesn't take long before she calls out in pleasure. I don't stop, though. I keep pounding into her at a delicious pace, getting closer to my own release. The feeling keeps building with every thrust, until at last, I come, emptying myself into her.

That was fucking fantastic.

Light streams in from the window, waking me in the morning. I roll over and see Brianne, still asleep next to me. I stayed with her last night, not wanting to leave her. We had an incredible time together. We just clicked—and the sex was amazing. Now, looking at her peacefully sleeping with her hair messed up, partially covering her face, an over-whelming feeling of contentment washes over me. This has been a fantastic weekend, and I'm sad that it's coming to an end today.

My flight leaves for Seattle at three o'clock this afternoon, so I have a little more time left to enjoy Vegas before I go. Everyone else in the wedding party is leaving at some point today as well, and I wonder what time Brianne's flight is. Perhaps we'll be on the same flight? That would be awesome. I'm not ready to say goodbye to her yet. Luckily, I don't have to do that for a while. Everyone is meeting for brunch this morning, so I have a few more hours to spend with Brianne.

Not wanting to wake her, I carefully and quietly roll over and get out of bed. I walk across the room toward the bathroom, and I suddenly hear Brianne's voice.

"Good morning," she says, her voice groggy. "Are you sneaking out?"

Stopping in my tracks, I turn and look at Brianne. "No, I'm just heading to the bathroom."

She chuckles. "Well, that's good." She leans up on her elbows and looks at me. "What time is it, anyway?"

"A quarter after nine," I reply. We stayed up late, having sex one more time before finally falling asleep. She definitely wore me out... and I'm still tired.

"Oh, wow," Brianne says. "That's a lot later than I expected." She sits up, swinging her legs over the side of the bed.

I shrug. "We have over an hour before we have to be downstairs. You've got plenty of time to get ready."

I admire her naked body. Her nipples stand at attention, begging to be touched. I thank the Lord we slept naked so I could be treated to this beautiful sight again this morning. I already had morning wood but looking at Brianne's sexy body makes me rock hard.

Brianne's eyes catch my hard-on, and her eyes widen a fraction.

"Like what you see?" I ask with a smirk on my face.

Brianne blushes, which isn't something she does often. I feel accomplished being able to make her blush.

"It's okay. He's a sight to behold," I say, gripping my dick in my hand.

Brianne bursts out in laughter. Should I feel insulted? My mouth turns down in a frown, and I release my grip on my cock.

She shakes her head, pulling herself back together. "No, no. I didn't mean to insult you and hurt your feelings." She pauses, then continues, "I really enjoyed your penis last night. Thanks for making me come."

Her words make me burst out in laughter, and after a beat, she joins in with me. At least I know we can joke around with each other. Brianne is a lot of fun to hang out with, and everything about the time we've spent together this weekend has been beyond all expectations. For starters, I never expected to spend time together and hit it off so well. But the sexual chemistry we have is undeniably spectacular––it's definitely something special. I can only hope I'll get another chance to be with Brianne, whether it's while we're still here in Vegas, or after we get home to Seattle.

I use the restroom, then gather my clothes strewn about the room.

"Are you leaving?" Brianne asks. She's in bed again, propped up with a pillow against
the headboard.

"Yeah, I need to take a shower and get ready for brunch."

She nods. "Okay. Well, I'll see you in about an hour and a half."

I put my shirt on, then walk around the bed to her. I lean over and kiss her sweetly on

the lips. "I really enjoyed last night." Running my hand down her cheek, I admire how beautiful she is, even first thing in the morning just after waking up.

"So did I," she replies, looking at me seductively through hooded eyes.

"What time do you fly back today?" I ask, curious if we'll have any time to hang out after brunch.

"Not until eight o'clock tonight. The late flight was cheaper."

"Oh, wow, you're staying late," I reply. "What are you going to do all day? Isn't everyone else leaving earlier?"

She shrugs. "I don't know yet. Probably gamble a bit, maybe do a little shopping."

The idea I had yesterday about staying in Vegas an extra night springs to mind. After the night we spent together, this idea is even more intriguing than it was before. I wonder if Brianne would be able to change her flight reservation and stay another day?

"How would you like to stay one more night?" I ask, hoping she'll say yes.

"Well, that would be amazing of course," she replies. "But it depends how much it would cost. Plus, I have to work at noon on Monday, so I'd have to fly out on an early flight Monday morning."

The wheels turn in my head. I want to make this happen. I'm not ready for my weekend fling with Brianne to end. "Let me see what I can do," I tell her.

"What?" She seems confused, but I ignore her and finish

gathering my things to leave. "Corey, what do you mean 'see what you can do?'"

I look at her and smile. "I don't know yet, but I'll let you know." I wink, then turn and head toward the door. Before leaving, I turn back toward her. "I'll see you in about an hour."

Brianne looks stunned, as if she can't quite believe what I said. As the door closes behind me, and I walk toward the elevator, I can only hope that I can make my idea a reality.

"Thank you so much for coming! We're so happy you could take a break from work and come down to celebrate with us." Chelsea hugs me, and I hug her in return.

"Of course, sis. I wouldn't miss your wedding."

After brunch, everyone congregates outside the restaurant to say goodbye to one another. Mostly everyone is heading to the airport now. The only ones who aren't are Carson's cousins, Brianne, and me. Once everyone leaves, I need to share my proposal with Brianne. During brunch, I had looked on my phone and found a flight with seats available that leaves Monday morning. I also checked The Caribbean's availability for tonight, and they have rooms. I just need to speak with the front desk to see if I can stay in my room another night, or if they'll have to move me to a different room.

Everybody finishes saying goodbye and then leaves. Brianne and I are left alone, and she looks at me expectantly.

"What time do you have to leave for the airport?" she asks.

My lips curls up in a smile. "Actually, I wanted to talk to you about that."

She cocks an eyebrow. "What do you mean?"

"I'd like to stay another day with you. I found a flight that leaves early tomorrow morning that still has available seats. You would be home in time to go to work."

Brianne's mouth drops open. "Wait... what? Are you serious?"

I nod. "Yes, I'm totally serious. I'm not ready to leave yet. I want another night with you."

Her eyebrows shoot upward. She's speechless.

"We'll just have to call the airline to switch our flights. I'll pay for the room, so you don't need to worry about that."

Brianne just stares at me for a moment, then shakes her head in disbelief. "I'm sorry... what? You want to stay in Vegas an extra night... with *me*?"

I chuckle. She's so damn cute. "Yes. I'm not ready to say goodbye to you yet."

I think I've stunned her. She doesn't say a word at first, she just continues to stare at me. Finally, she opens her mouth, only to close it again. But then she does speak. "Um, that's very generous of you. Are you sure?"

I nod emphatically. "More than anything. Let's stay another night together."

Brianne rubs her forehead, and I think she's seriously considering my proposition. Then she drops her hand and says, "Okay. Let's do it!"

Smiling wide, I pull her into a hug. "Thank you."

We decide to sit in a bar so we can change our flight reservations. Then, I go to the hotel reservation desk to ask about extending my stay for one night. Luckily, I'm able to keep the same room so I don't have to move. Once everything is settled, Brianne and I go up to her room to move her things to mine. Then, we head back down to the casino to have a little fun gambling.

However, I already feel as if I won the jackpot.

# Brianne

## NINE

"That was fucking amazing!" I can't wipe the smile from my face as Corey and I walk away from the zip line ride we just took over Fremont Street. We've decided to leave the strip and go downtown for some fun, and we certainly found it. Soaring over the street was exhilarating. Something I never thought I'd experience.

"Yeah, it was," Corey agrees. "What a rush!"

"What do you want to do now?" I ask, wondering what other fun we can have together.

"I don't know. Wanna do a little gambling?"

"Of course!" Considering I'm up a total of five hundred bucks this weekend, I can afford to play a little.

We walk into the nearest casino, the Four Queens. The vibe in these older casinos is different from the ones on the strip. They're older, smaller, and it feels as if we've taken a step back in time.

"Let's play blackjack," Corey suggests as we walk by the tables.

"I've never played before," I admit.

Corey stops and looks at me with a wicked smile. "Well, you're going to learn."

Something about the way he says that turns me on. "Are you going to teach me?" I ask seductively.

Corey smirks. "You know I will. Come on."

I follow him to a blackjack table, and he explains the rules to me as we watch others play. I get the hang of it pretty quickly. Corey notices the table next to us is open, so he takes my hand and leads me over to it.

We take our seats, and the dealer welcomes us. I'm a little nervous to play, but I'm also excited to give it a try. We place our bets, and the dealer deals the cards.

My cards equal twenty-one.

"Holy shit," Corey says, shaking his head. "Beginner's luck?"

I laugh. "I guess so!"

Of course, I'm the winner, and the dealer takes our cards and gives me my winning chips. Then, we place our bets for the next round. This time I hit nineteen, but I'm still the winner.

"Woohoo!" I throw my hands in the air in celebration. "This is awesome!"

Corey laughs. "You're off to a good start there, babe."

I take a double take at him. The way he calls me *babe* takes me by surprise, but I also like the sound of it. I smile but try to hide the fact that his choice of words has an effect on me.

We continue playing blackjack for quite a while. By the time we're finished, I come out as the big winner between the two of us. I lose a few games, but I win most of them, bringing my winning total of the weekend up to nearly seven hundred bucks.

As we walk away from the table, Corey asks, "Are you getting hungry? I'm starving."

"I hadn't thought about it before, but I could eat. I guess it's been awhile since brunch."

"Yeah, it's already dinner time," Corey says as we walk through the casino. "We should probably collect our winnings first, though."

We approach the casino cashier and collect our money, and Corey asks where the nearest restaurant is. The cashier recommends a good place to eat in the casino called Hugo's Cellar, so we take her advice and follow the directions she gave. Once we find it, I immediately like the looks of the brick walls and how it's situated downstairs as if we're really going to a cellar. Our luck continues as they have a table available, which apparently is usually hard to get without making a reservation first.

All through dinner, Corey and I talk like old friends. We reminisce about when we were younger––memories we both have from times I was at their house to hang out with Chelsea. We also share memories of teachers from the middle and high school we attended. Although we never had any classes together since he was two grades behind me, we did have some of the same teachers. It's a fun walk down memory lane, and I find myself enjoying Corey's company even more than before. I'm finding that he's not only a nice guy who I'm strongly attracted to, but we also have a lot in common, just as Chelsea had told me we would.

Dinner is delicious, and it occurs to me that the ambience inside Hugo's Cellar is also––dare I say it––*romantic.*

Although Corey and I have had almost every meal together the past couple of days, this is the first time we're eating alone. It almost feels as if we're on a date together... but I refuse to let myself go down that road. Those are not the types of thoughts I need to have. Neither Corey nor I are ones to have relationships. This is just a fun weekend fling we're having together in Vegas. We're both open to having a good time with no strings attached. What better place to do that than in the City of Sin?

"Hey, remember that time you spent an entire week at our house?" Corey asks. "I think your mom was out of town or something."

"Of course I do," I reply, taking a sip of my cosmo. "Chelsea and I were juniors, and my mom went to Mexico with her boyfriend at the time. I was bitter I didn't get to go, but then Chelsea and I had a lot of fun that week. Why do you ask?"

Corey chuckles. He looks down and rubs his chin, as if he's contemplating something. Then, he looks back up at me. "Well, that was the first time I saw boobs in person."

My jaw drops. I had totally forgotten about this.

"Do you remember?" he asks.

How did I forget about this? The memory comes flooding back, and I slowly nod. "Ummm, yeah, I do. I got up in the middle of the night to use the bathroom. I was tired and not thinking, and although the bathroom door was shut, I just went ahead and opened it."

"I should've locked the door, I guess," Corey says. "Of course, if I had, we wouldn't have had that moment together."

I can't help but smile at Corey. Then, I continue, "I walked in on you getting out of the shower. You were totally naked, and I saw your dick." Thinking back on it now, I remember thinking how scrawny Corey was... except his penis wasn't. In fact, if I remember correctly, he had a hard-on. "By the way, did you have an erection?" I ask him.

Corey guffaws, shaking his head. "Well, yeah..." He leans in closer and lowers his voice. "I had just jerked off in the shower."

I gasp, covering my mouth with my hand. "You did? You must've been so embarrassed when I walked in!"

"Well..." Corey smirks. "Wanna know a secret?"

Nodding, I wonder what he's going to divulge.

"I had the biggest crush on you."

My heart pounds in my chest. I think I know where he's going with this, but I want to hear him say it.

"I couldn't stop thinking about you being in the room next to me. Why do you think I got up in the middle of the night to take a shower?" He scoffs. "I couldn't sleep, so I decided to get up and take a shower... and jerk off while thinking about you."

Although this happened a decade ago when we were only teenagers, I still can't help but be turned on, knowing that Corey was so strongly attracted to me back then. And knowing what happened after I walked into the bathroom makes what was a forgettable memory for me so much hotter now.

"Then, you walked in while I was drying myself with the towel," he continues, "and you practically made my fantasy become a reality."

I nod, slowly. "I remember walking in and seeing you. I was shocked and embarrassed at first. But then you just stood there, looking at me. You didn't cover yourself up or anything, and I figured the only way to make the awkward moment less awkward for you was to––"

"Show me your tits," Corey says, finishing my sentence. He chuckles once, his eyes burning into me. He's so damn sexy.

I laugh. "Yeah... a little 'you showed me yours, so I'll show you mine,' I guess."

"You have no idea how much that turned me on, though," Corey says. "When you lifted your shirt up and showed me your breasts, I nearly combusted."

Something he said earlier pops in my mind again. "*Mine* were the first real boobs you ever saw?"

He nods. "Yep. That was you."

My eyebrows shoot up in surprise. "Wow. I feel so... *honored.*"

Corey smiles, and my lower belly muscles clench.

"You were my fantasy for quite a while." His words shock me. "I mean, obviously I had a crush on you before that night, but after that incident, I was practically obsessed with you. Whenever you came over to our house, I had to hide my hard-on. That's why I was so shy around you, Brianne."

My mouth falls open again. His confession is not only surprising, but it also makes me want him more. Knowing he had such strong feelings for me back then makes me wonder how strong his feelings are for me now. Again, I wonder if this is just a weekend fling for him, or if it means more.

But I want to stay in the moment, not worry about feelings. Sharing his secret has turned this into a hot, intimate moment for us, and I don't want to ruin that. I want Corey, and after all we've done together this weekend, I want tonight to be the cherry on top––the best night we've shared, and possibly *ever* will share together.

I lean in toward Corey so only he can hear me. "I want to take you to a strip club."

He sucks in a breath, and I can tell he's turned on by my suggestion. We had discussed visiting a strip club together a couple of nights ago, but it never happened. The fantasies I had of us getting a lap dance together make my clit throb, and I know without a doubt that Corey and I are about to have one hot night out in Vegas together. I'm going to enjoy every second of it––and I won't hold anything back.

After a short Uber ride, we make our way into the strip club. Topless women are dancing on platforms scattered about the club. Some have G-strings on, but some are totally naked. There's one woman on the mainstage as well, putting on a show as she twirls around a pole. Corey and I find a table near the stage and watch the beautiful blond stripper as she bends backwards, one hand still holding onto the pole as her other hand toys with her breast.

"This is a nice place," Corey says as he rests his arm on the back of my chair.

As I look around, I notice I'm not the only woman in the audience, but there are mostly men. All of the strippers are gorgeous. "Yeah, it seems more upscale than others I've visited before," I say.

Corey turns his head toward me. "Do these women turn you on?"

A smile slowly spreads on my face. "Yeah, they do."

Corey blows air out of his mouth as he turns his head back toward the stage. "Fuck, that's a sexy thought."

"What is?" I ask, wondering what he's thinking.

He turns back to me. "Picturing you getting a lap dance," he says, his voice gravelly.

I lean in and whisper in his ear, "I want us to get a lap dance together."

Corey wipes his hand down his face, then adjusts the crotch of his jeans. "Fuck, Brianne," he says, and I revel in the fact that I've turned him on even more.

A topless waitress approaches and asks what we'd like to drink. We place our orders, and then she walks away.

The stripper on stage ends her routine, and the announcer says, "Let's give it up for Star! Up next, you're all in for a treat... Vega is taking the stage!"

The audience cheers, and as Star leaves the stage, another stripper walks on. The music changes, and as "Pony" by Ginuwine plays, Vega dances sexily in front of us. She's wearing a white lacy bra and matching thong, her long, curly hair bouncing as she moves her body. I find her even more beautiful than Star, and her body is to die for. I wish I were in as good shape as her. Maybe I need to take pole dancing classes to look like that.

Corey and I watch as Vega dances, and before long, she removes her bra. I suck in a breath. Her breasts are perfect. She's probably a D cup, and her nipples are a rosy pink. As she struts in our direction on the stage, her hands fondle her breasts, and her eyes catch mine. She continues her routine while keeping eye contact with me––or maybe she's looking at Corey––but either way, it makes me wet. She pinches both of her nipples, and her head falls back in pleasure. Then, her hands skim down her stomach to her panties, and she teases taking them off. She looks forward again, looking directly at us once more before turning around and bending over, showing off her tight ass.

Our waitress returns with our drinks, and Corey and I both take long sips. The cosmo here is much better than the one I had at dinner, and I find it easy to drink. I already feel the effects of the alcohol I've had over the course of the night and being in the strip club adds to my buzz. It's exciting, hot, and I'm buzzing with the anticipation of what could happen.

Vega continues dancing, still making eye contact with me from time to time. She never takes her thong off, unlike Star who had gotten completely naked. But she's still one of the sexiest women I've ever seen, and I wonder if she gives private dances.

Once her time on stage ends, Corey and I clap for her, and I notice her look back at us one more time before leaving the stage. Maybe she'll come out on the floor? I hope we see her again.

"She was good," Corey says in my ear. "I liked her."

"I did, too," I say. "I wonder if we could get a private dance later?"

Corey cocks an eyebrow. "That would be fucking hot."

The next dancer comes out, and while she's nice to watch as well, I'm not as attracted to her as I was with Vega. Still, she dances nicely and puts on a good show. She also takes everything off, showing the audience her bare pussy.

Corey and I both finish our drinks, and our waitress returns to ask if we want another.

"Yes, please," Corey says. "And––how do we go about getting a private dance?"

The waitress smiles. "You just have to ask. Is there a particular dancer you want?"

Corey looks at me and smiles, then looks back at our waitress. "Vega," he says, and I instantly smile.

It takes awhile, but after we finish our second drink, a beautiful curly-haired woman wearing a black silky bra and matching thong is suddenly standing in front of us. Vega. I find it interesting that she wore white on stage, and now she's wearing black. Is she more innocent on stage than in private? Jesus, I don't know what I'm in for if that's the case.

"Hi," she says with a smile. "Did you two order a private dance?"

Corey and I glance at each other, then back at her. "Yes," he answers for us.

"Follow me," she says.

We both stand and follow her to a back room. My heart pounds in my chest with anticipation. What's going to happen in this private room? What exactly is included in a private dance at this club?

We enter a room with low lighting and music playing, just like the rest of the club. In the middle, there's a couch, and a few feet in front of the couch is a stripper pole.

"Have a seat," Vega says as she walks around the couch toward the pole.

Corey and I look at one another, then do as she says. We sit close to one another, our legs touching, and Corey puts his arm around me.

"Are you two a couple?" she asks as she circles her hips.

"Um, not exactly," Corey says. "But we're together."

*Interesting explanation.* Although, I suppose for all intents and purposes, that's an accurate way to describe us for now.

"And do you both want a lap dance, or just one of you while the other watches?"

Corey and I glance at each other once again. I cock an eyebrow at him, then turn back to Vega. "We both want a dance," I say.

She moves toward us, slow and sexy. "Okay," she says. "Just so you know, there are no rules in here, so anything goes."

*Holy shit.*

Vega dances just inches away from us. It's not long before she reaches behind her back and unhooks her bra. She drags the straps down her arms, then tosses it to the side. She leans over Corey, snaking her body up toward him, her perky breasts skimming his face. Then, she takes a step toward me and does the same. Her nipple touches my cheek, sending goosebumps down my body. She continues dancing in front of us, then turns and acts as if she's going to sit on Corey's lap, but she moves her hips back up, showing off her ass. Then, like before, she does the same thing to me.

When she turns to face us again, she moves her hips as her hands move up her body to her breasts. As she touches herself, she looks at me and asks, "Do you want me to take my thong off?"

My belly stirs with excitement at how dirty and hot this is getting. I nod, unable to take my eyes off her to consult Corey first. "Yes." I swallow hard.

She winks at me and continues dancing but doesn't remove her underwear right away. Instead, she crawls onto Corey's lap, her leg pressing between us. I watch as she gives him one hell of a lap dance, grinding her body against his, shoving her breasts in his face. Corey had removed his arm from my shoulder and now has both hands firmly grasping her ass. Vega is beyond sexy, and it's driving me wild watching her give Corey a lap dance.

After a while, she stands again and dances in front of us for a bit. That's when she rolls her thong down her legs and takes it off. My jaw hits the floor as she continues dancing, completely naked. She has no hair, so her slit is visible, as well as a tiny tattoo of a heart just above it. When she moves toward me and climbs onto my lap, my mouth goes dry.

She straddles my lap and grinds against me. "You can touch," she says in my ear. "Give your boyfriend a good show."

I gulp. Should I? It's not as if I've never done anything with a girl before, but I've never put on a show for someone else to watch. However, I'm so fucking hot right now, and Vega's plump breasts are right in my face... I'm not sure I want to waste this opportunity to have some dirty fun with Corey. That's why we came here after all, isn't it? I was the one who suggested going to a strip club in the first place, and this is my fantasy come true. It's not the time to hold back. I need to let my inhibitions go.

Placing my hands on her hips, I slowly glide them up the side of her body until I reach her breasts. She arches her back, sticking her breasts out toward me, so I go for it––I wrap my lips around one of her taut nipples and roll the other between my fingers. Vega moans, and I hear Corey next to me whisper, "Holy shit."

I turn my head to look at him, and he's nearly salivating. I cup her breast closest to him and say, "Want some?"

Corey wipes his hand down his face, then moves closer. "Fuck yeah, I do," he says before sucking her nipple in his mouth. My clit throbs as Corey and I watch one another sucking on Vega's tits. It's fucking hot as hell, and I wonder just how much will happen here in this private room with Vega.

Vega grinds her pussy against my lap, and Corey takes my hand in his, lifting it toward Vega's slit. "Touch her," he says.

Corey holds the top of my hand, guiding it in touching Vega's pussy. My fingers feel her wet folds and rub back and forth as Corey guides me. She lets out another sexy moan, seemingly enjoying what we're doing to her. Corey moves my hand up, and I find her clit, rubbing it in circles.

"Keep going," Corey says, taking his hand off mine. "I want to watch."

Corey relaxes against the couch, stretching both arms across the back. I look at Vega's face. This is it. We're going to give Corey a show.

"Can I undo your top?" she asks as she unties the straps of my halter top that are tied together behind my neck. If she unties it, she could just pull my top down, and I'm not wearing a bra.

I nod, and she loosens the straps. My finger continues to rub her pussy as she does it, but as soon as she pulls my shirt down and the cool air hits my bare breasts, I freeze. This is really happening right now.

Vega rubs her breasts against mine, and I nearly come when our nipples touch. "Fuck," Corey says, and I look over at him, adjusting the fly of his jeans.

Vega notices and says, "Do you need a hand?"

Holy shit.

"Nah. I just want to watch you two." I look over to see Corey rubbing his bulge over his jeans.

Vega leans down and sucks my nipple in her mouth. My head falls back, enjoying her touch. I continue rubbing her clit, and she grinds against my finger. "I'm gonna come," she says, then switches to suck on my other nipple.

I turn my head and look at Corey. He's still rubbing his dick over his jeans, and I wonder why he's not taking it out to stroke it. He looks completely turned on watching us, though, which spurs me on. I increase my pressure on Vega's clit and within seconds, she comes, loudly. Her body shakes as she moans, and my fingers get soaked as I continue to rub her pussy.

Corey licks his lips, and suddenly, all I want is to be with him. Alone. Sure, Vega is beyond sexy, and I'm having fun with her, but I also want Corey more than anything right now.

Vega stands and retrieves a hand towel from a nearby table. "Here you go," she says as she hands it to me. As I wipe my fingers, she dances in front of Corey again. He's watching her with hooded eyes, and although I enjoy watching her move, I also suddenly feel a pang of jealousy. *I* want to touch Corey. I want him to touch *me*. As much fun as this private dance has been, I think it's time for it to end. All I want is Corey.

Corey watches Vega dance, but he doesn't touch her. She rubs her breasts against him, but he doesn't take advantage of her. Instead, he turns his head and looks at me. "I want you," he mouths, and my stomach flip flops in excitement. He wants me, too.

I pull my shirt back up and tie the straps behind my neck as I watch Vega continue to dance for Corey. When she notices I've put my shirt back on, she says, "Are we done already?"

"I really enjoyed that," I say, not wanting to insult her. "But I think it's time for us to go."

She smiles, then stands and stops dancing. "I really enjoyed that, too. Thanks for the good time." She winks at me, then bends over to pick up her underwear.

Corey and I look at one another and stand to leave. He pulls his wallet out of his pocket and gives Vega a hefty tip.

"Thanks, hon," she says with another wink.

Corey takes my hand in his, and then we leave.

# *Corey*

## TEN

G od. Damn.

That was one of the hottest scenes I've ever watched play out in front of me before. Brianne and Vega sucking each other's nipples, rubbing them together... and then Brianne made her come... I nearly came in my pants just from watching. However, I forced myself to restrain from whipping my dick out and stroking it. I knew we could've taken things further with Vega if we wanted to, but that's just it... I didn't want to. Sure, it was a complete turn on. But at one point as I watched Brianne and Vega getting each other off, I started to feel something. It wasn't jealousy, but that's the closest thing I can compare it to. I just wanted Brianne all to myself.

Thank God Brianne was on the same page as me. As soon as we left, I requested an Uber, which picked us up within a few minutes. Now, we're riding back to The Caribbean, barely able to keep our hands off each other in the backseat. Brianne sits in the middle, so my arm is around her shoulders. My hand fits nicely inside her halter top, my fingers toying with her nipple. Her hand is between my legs, rubbing my cock over my jeans. I can't fucking wait to get to our hotel room.

Luckily, it's a short drive to The Caribbean. We exit the Uber, then hurry inside, bypassing the casino and making our way to the elevators. Unfortunately, we're not alone on the elevator, though. I've been hoping to pin her against the wall and kiss her senselessly as we ride up to the tenth floor.

The moment the elevator stops, and we get off, we hurry to the room. I can hardly contain my excitement; I want Brianne so badly.

As soon as I unlock the door and we enter the room, all bets are off, and it's obvious that Brianne has the same idea. We reach for each other, crashing together as my lips find hers. "God, I want you," I say as we make our way to the bed.

Our hands fumble as we rip each other's clothes off. As soon as she's lying naked in front of me, I crawl on the bed, settle between her legs, and lick her sweet pussy.

"Yes! Just like that!" Brianne's hands grip my hair as I pleasure her with my tongue. She's soaking wet, and by the way she's responding to me, I don't think it'll take long for her to come.

I focus on licking her clit as I insert two fingers, and she bucks against me.

"Corey... yes... don't stop." Hearing her say my name makes me rock hard, and I can't wait to be inside her. I need to make her come first, though. I rub her inner wall as I suck on her clit, and she moans in pleasure. "I'm coming!" she calls, pulling my hair.

As she recovers, I stand to get a condom. Then I crawl back onto the bed and position myself over her. Before I slide inside her, though, I'm struck by how beautiful she is. Some of her hair is covering her eye, so I softly brush it out of the way. Brianne looks up at me, and my heart stands still. This weekend has turned out to be so different from what I expected it to be. If someone had told me I'd be in this position right now, hovering over Brianne Hamilton, about to have sex with her for the *second* time, I would've laughed in their face. This is a fantasy I've had since middle school, and I never expected it to come true.

But here I am, looking deeply into Brianne's beautiful eyes. I lower my mouth to hers and kiss her sweetly. I take this kiss nice and slow, and Brianne wraps her arms around my neck, holding me close. Our tongues glide against each other, but we don't hurry this kiss. There's something about this kiss that shifts our entire night. Before this, everything was hot and heavy. Now, it feels sweeter... as if there's more emotion behind this kiss.

*Maybe there is.*

"I need you," Brianne says, pulling her lips away just long enough to say it.

That's all I need to hear. I slide my cock inside her until I'm fully seated, balls deep in her tight pussy. I rear back and fuck her, but I don't rush it. I go at a slow pace, reveling in how good it feels. Brianne's fingernails dig into my back, and she moans in pleasure. Looking down at her again, I become overwhelmed with an emotion I'm not used to having when I have sex. I don't know what it is, but I know one thing-- my feelings for Brianne are stronger than they should be.

I need to shove these thoughts aside right now, though. I can't worry about my feelings while I'm in the middle of fucking Brianne. I roll us over so she's on top, and I can watch how sexy she is while she rides me. She slides up and down on my cock at the perfect pace, and it drives me closer to release. I want to watch Brianne come again before I do, though. I slide my finger between us to rub her clit, hoping to help her come sooner. It works. Before I know it, I feel her muscles clench around my cock, and Brianne calls out in ecstasy. Seeing her come undone sets me off, and I call out as I pour myself into her.

I wake in the middle of the night, Brianne still asleep next to me. Nature calls. I get up and use the restroom, and when I get back to bed, I look at my phone to see what time it is. Three thirty-five. My alarm is set to go off in two hours. Our flight home leaves at nine o'clock, so there's no sleeping in for us, unfortunately.

As I look at my phone, I also see a text message from Seline. I hadn't heard from her since Friday night, and I thought maybe she'd taken the hint this time. However, it appears that's not the case. She sends me a selfie, as well as tells me she's been thinking about me all weekend.

Shit.

I set my phone down on the nightstand, then lie back down in bed. I guess I'll have to be more straightforward with Seline, so she gets the hint that I'm no longer interested in her. There's only one woman I'm actually interested in right now, and she's lying in bed next to me.

Will this be the last time Brianne and I ever sleep together? I hope not. I don't know how Brianne feels, but I'd like to see her again back home in Tacoma. Who knows what'll happen once we're back, though. The magic of Sin City may wear off as we go back to our regular lives, and we may never go out together again. It's possible she doesn't want to continue where we left off here, and I'll have to respect that. I guess only time will tell what happens between Brianne and me.

~

When I wake in the morning, Brianne is already up and getting ready in the bathroom. I drag myself out of bed and pick up my clothes off the floor to pack in my suitcase. We have to leave in forty-five minutes to get to the airport in time. I'm exhausted and relieved that I took today off from work.

The bathroom door opens, and Brianne walks out. Her hair is still wet, but she's dressed and has her makeup done already. "Oh, hey," she says nonchalantly as she walks across the room to her suitcase to put her toiletries away.

"Good morning," I say.

Something about the way she looked at me and just said 'oh, hey' so casually feels off. I'm getting a completely different vibe from her than I did last night, or the rest of this weekend for that matter. What's going on?

"Did you sleep good?" I ask, hoping my instincts are off.

She nods, then heads back toward the bathroom. "Did you?" she asks.

"Yeah, I guess so," I reply. I don't like this feeling. Brianne seems cold and distant.

I walk into the bathroom. "Do you mind if I take a shower?"

"Go ahead," she says, picking up more of her things and walking past me to put them in her suitcase.

What the fuck is going on?

I don't want to dwell on it, though. I can't. From the moment this weekend started, it was clear that Brianne and I were just having a good time together. It was a fling. Nothing more. And now, the weekend is over, and so are we.

I need to get over this. Brianne and I were never a *real* thing. She's just like me—she likes to party and have fun, and she doesn't do relationships. We're players. Not relationship material.

Forty minutes later, we're both ready to leave. We gather our things and head down to the lobby. We're totally silent in the elevator. We're alone this time, but I can't pin her against the wall and kiss her like I wanted to last night. She's barely speaking to me this morning, and she'd probably punch me if I tried to kiss her right now. The worst part is, I don't understand why. I have no idea why Brianne is acting so distant today. It's as if she wants nothing to do with me anymore. As confused as I am, I don't want to open a can of worms and question her about it. I'll just go along with it. We'll be back home soon and can go our separate ways, back to our own lives. Vegas can be a great memory.

We take an Uber to the airport, then check in for our flight and check our luggage. As we wait in the security line, we barely speak. Everything we say to one another has to do with our flight home. We don't discuss last night or anything else. I have a pit in my stomach, wondering what the hell happened. Did I say or do something wrong? Or, does she regret what we did last night?

Things are awkward, and I don't know what to do about it. Originally, when we changed our flight, I was glad we were able to book the same flight but sad our seats weren't next to each other. Now, though, I'm relieved we won't be sitting by each other. Brianne is definitely not wanting to be around me right now. I just wish I knew why.

After we land at SeaTac, I make my way off the plane, hoping that Brianne waited for me when she got off since she was sitting several rows ahead of me. To my surprise, she's there, waiting for me. I smile when I see her.

"Hey, you," I say, hoping that maybe things will be better between us now.

She cracks a smile, but it's not the same as she smiled this weekend. She doesn't look as happy as she was. "Baggage claim is this way," she says, pointing in the direction we need to go.

We walk together to baggage claim, then wait in silence for our luggage. She's checking something on her phone, seemingly keeping busy so she can ignore me. Nothing has changed since we left Vegas.

After we retrieve our bags, we walk together toward the exit. Yesterday, I offered to drive her home since I left my truck in the long-term parking lot. Maybe she'll open up more on the drive home?

Nope. Nothing. We talk a little, but it's all surface-level conversation. She gives me directions to her apartment, and once we get there, I offer to help her carry her bags inside, but she turns me down.

"I'm fine. You don't need to park and get out."

"Are you sure? I don't mind at all," I say, and it's the truth. As strange as she's acting now, I still like Brianne. I wish I knew what was wrong.

"No, it's fine. I'm kind of in a hurry since I have to get to work," she says. "Thanks for the ride, though. I really appreciate it."

Before she gets out of the truck, I reach for her hand,

getting her attention. She turns to look at me, and suddenly, there are a million things I'd like to say to her. I settle with asking her just one thing. "Is everything okay?"

"Yeah, I'm fine," she says. "I'm just really tired and bummed that I have to work. Thanks for the fun weekend. I really enjoyed staying an extra night with you." She pulls her hand away from mine and gets out of my truck. Before closing the door, she looks back at me. "I really did have a great time."

What the fuck? Why is she acting like this? If she had a great time with me, why is she acting so distant?

She closes the door, then opens the back passenger door to get her bags. "Thanks, Corey. See 'ya around."

Before I can respond, she closes the door. I watch as she wheels her luggage to her apartment and unlocks her door. She gives me a little wave before she goes inside, and I'm left with more questions that I'll probably never get answered.

# Brianne

## ELEVEN

It's been a week since I flew to Vegas for what was to be a fun weekend celebrating my best friend's wedding. It turned into so much more, though. Of course, it was an amazing weekend with my friends, and Chelsea's wedding was wonderful. Everything that happened with Corey, though, was totally unexpected. It was fun, exciting, and hot as fucking hell. I thought for sure we were developing real feelings for each other.

And then I saw his phone, and all thoughts of us continuing our fling after Vegas were crushed.

I wasn't snooping. He got up in the middle of the night to use the bathroom, and when he came back to bed, he looked at his phone. He didn't realize I had awoken as well. Lying behind him in bed, I could see his phone screen, and I saw the selfie he received from a beautiful blonde. I know women don't send texts to guys unless there's something going on between them. I was instantly reminded of what Chelsea had warned me about her brother--Corey's a player. He just wants to have a good time with women, not

106

date or have serious relationships. Seeing another woman texting him pulled me back down to reality. We were only having a weekend fling together. Nothing more.

But the way that made me feel was unexpected. I felt hurt. Used. *Played.* The things we did together just hours before were fucking intimate. He made me feel as if he really cared for me. When we had sex, it felt like there was more emotion behind it. The way he looked into my eyes, the way he touched me... I truly felt like there was a chance for us to be more. I've never felt this way before, and I actually thought this was a turning point in my life.

I was fucking dumb.

And now, four days after we flew back home, I've only heard from Corey once. On Tuesday, he sent me a text asking if I was doing okay. I replied, telling him I was fine, and I hoped he was doing well, too. He said he was, and that was it. I haven't had any more communication with him since.

It's Friday night, and I've just gotten off work. Chelsea has invited me over to her and Carson's house for a late dinner, and I've accepted. I haven't seen them since last weekend, so it'll be nice to get together.

As I drive to their place, I can't stop thinking about Corey. I wonder if Chelsea has talked to her brother at all this week, and if so, did he tell her anything that happened between us? God, I hope he wouldn't tell her *everything* we did, but it would be nice if she could give me some insight as to how her brother feels about me.

I find a place to park, then make my way to Chelsea and Carson's apartment. I knock on the door, and within seconds, Chelsea opens the door. "Hi!" She greets me with a wide smile. "Come on in!"

"Hey, girlfriend," I say as I step inside, stopping to give her a hug. Then, I kick my shoes off and walk into the living area. Carson is in the kitchen making drinks.

"Hi, Brianne. Would you like a margarita?" he asks.

"Of course," I reply. "I could definitely use a drink."

Chelsea and I sit on the couches in the living room.

"So... did you have a good week at work?" she asks.

"Yeah, I guess. Nothing too awful happened," I say with a laugh.

Carson walks in and hands us each a margarita. "Thanks," we both say to him.

I take a sip, and it's perfect. "This is delicious, Carson. Just what I need."

"I'm glad you like it," he says as he goes back in the kitchen to do something else, leaving Chelsea and me alone to talk.

"So... I have to admit I had an ulterior motive when I invited you over."

My stomach drops, and I look at my friend, waiting for her to say more. My mind races with possibilities of what she's going to say, but my gut tells me it has to do with her brother.

"Corey told me about the extra night you two stayed in Vegas together," Chelsea says, cutting right to the chase.

"Oh," I reply, wondering just how much he actually told her. Hopefully, he edited our trip to the strip club out of their conversation. I take a drink of my margarita, then look down at the glass as I set it on my lap.

"He's really confused," she says, and my eyes fly up to meet hers.

"What?" Now *I'm* confused.

"He said you guys had a great night together, and then

all of a sudden, you were distant in the morning. You barely wanted to speak to him."

I stare at my friend for a moment, trying to understand what Corey's point of view might be. Yeah, I was distant. Yeah, we barely spoke. But why should he care when he's got Blondie texting him selfies of herself? Obviously, he's not looking for anything other than a good time.

I clear my throat, then say, "Well, I happened to see something on his phone that made me think he wasn't that interested in me."

Chelsea's eyebrows knit inward. "What did you see?"

I take another drink of my margarita. How much do I want to confess to Chelsea? If I let her in on my true feelings for Corey, that could backfire. She may be my best friend, but she's also Corey's sister. I don't know if she would want the two of us together. Sure, she gave us her blessing for a fun weekend in Vegas, but she knows how I am with men. Would she want me in a relationship with Corey?

"Look," I start, trying to avoid getting too deep into this, "I just happened to see a text he got from another girl. It reminded me that he's just looking for a good time and nothing more."

"And... were *you* looking for something more?"

Fuck. She caught that. I should've been more careful with my words.

"I'm not looking for anything," I say, then take another gulp of my drink.

Chelsea's eyes soften. "Brianne, I don't know who was texting Corey or what that was all about, but I do know that he likes you. He was confused about the way you were acting, and his feelings are hurt. I just want to know if you were actually developing feelings for him. Because he seems to think you were... until your whole demeanor changed when you flew back home."

I'm stunned and don't know what to say. I look down at the glass in my hand. I hurt Corey's feelings? *Me*? What about him? My feelings were crushed when I saw him looking at that text.

"Brianne," Chelsea says, and I look up at her. "I think you and Corey should talk. There seems to be a misunderstanding between the two of you."

I shake my head. "I don't know. Did Corey actually tell you that I hurt his feelings?"

She nods. "Yes. He told me he hoped you two would go out again sometime, but after the way you acted, he didn't think you wanted anything to do with him anymore."

Not only am I surprised, but I'm also confused. Why would he care so much if he's got other bitches texting him? Like Chelsea told me before, he's a player. Well, I know his type because I'm a player myself. We don't get attached. We like playing the field. So, why does he care so much about me all of a sudden?

"Did he really tell you he likes me?" I ask, hoping she can shed more light on this situation.

"Yes, he did. He said he was starting to develop feelings and wanted to see you again... but then things changed." She shrugs. "I've actually never seen my brother quite like this about a woman before."

Well, shit. Maybe I got it all wrong? Maybe the text he received didn't mean anything to him after all?

I rub my forehead with my hand. What should I do now? Text him? Call him? Ask Chelsea where he lives and drive over to his house?

Just then, there's a knock on the door. Chelsea's eyes

shoot up as she stands to go answer it. "Please don't be mad," she says, putting her hands together as if she's praying. "But I also invited Corey over."

"What?" I shriek. My face falls, and my heart rate increases as I panic about seeing him already. I haven't had time to digest all the information I just learned, and now I'm supposed to see him face to face?

Chelsea puts her hand on the doorknob, then looks back at me. "He doesn't know you're here either."

Great! He'll be in shock, too. Why did Chelsea think this was a good idea?

She opens the door, and there he is. The man I'm attracted to more than any other. He doesn't see me yet, though. My heart is beating so hard, I can hear it in my ears. She has set us up. She planned this to get us back together. I'm not sure if I should be furious with Chelsea or so happy I could kiss her. My thoughts are jumbled and all over the place, I don't know what to think right now. The only thing that's clear in my mind is that my attraction to Corey is still strong.

Corey walks in, and the moment his eyes meet mine, he stops in his tracks. "What?" he says, stunned to see me here.

Chelsea walks past him. "Yeah... so I invited Bri over, too. I thought you two should talk."

Corey stares at me for a moment before following his sister into the living room. Instead of sitting next to me, he sits on the other side, next to Chelsea.

"Hey, Corey," Carson says from the kitchen. "Want a margarita?"

"Sure," he replies, keeping his eyes on mine. "I could use a drink."

Chelsea looks back and forth between us for a second, then says, "Okay, you two. Here's the deal."

My head snaps toward her, as does Corey's. She's going to tell us what the deal is? What the hell is going on here?

"I know for a fact that you like each other," Chelsea says. "I could see it while we were in Vegas. The chemistry between you two was palpable. Anyone who was at our wedding could sense it."

My jaw drops. There's no way we were that obvious... were we?

Chelsea continues, "And I also know that there's been a big misunderstanding between the two of you, and if you'd just talk to each other and listen, you might realize how silly it all is."

"It's not silly," Corey says, his voice flat.

"Okay, you're right. Silly isn't the right word... how about stupid?"

Corey and I both roll our eyes at Chelsea.

"Whatever," Corey says, shaking his head.

Chelsea ignores him and continues talking, "Corey, who was the girl you received a text from the night before you two left?"

Corey looks dumbfounded. "How the hell do you know about that?"

Chelsea rolls her eyes. "Because Bri saw it, dumbass. Tell us who she is."

Corey glares at his sister but surprisingly answers her question anyway. "She's a girl I went out with a couple of times who couldn't take the hint that I wasn't interested. She kept texting me even though I wasn't interested in seeing her anymore. I ended up calling her after I got back to town and let her down easy, so she's out of the picture now."

My heart is in my throat. The blonde didn't mean anything to him? Fuckity fuck, fuck, fuck. This was just a huge misunderstanding? I feel like a complete idiot. I'm not good at relationships... I've never been in one, so how could I be?

"Well, Brianne saw the selfie she sent you behind your back when you looked at the text and thought she was someone special to you. *That's* why she became so distant the next morning."

Corey looks at me and I look at him. "Is that true?" he asks.

Nodding my head, I suddenly feel like the biggest idiot on the face of the earth. How could I be so dumb? I jumped to conclusions, and where did it get me? Acting like a total bitch to the man I am developing feelings for. I pushed him away.

"I'm sorry," I say, my voice barely louder than a whisper. I take a deep breath. "When I saw her text, it made me feel like you were just using me. Like our time together in Vegas was just an insignificant fling to you." Suddenly, I feel as if this is a conversation we need to have in private, not in front of Chelsea and Carson. "Can we go somewhere else to talk, just you and me?"

Corey's features soften, and his shoulders relax a little. "Yeah. I think that's a good idea."

Chelsea pipes in, "Yes, I think that's a good idea, too. We can have dinner another night. I just wanted to get you two talking again."

I stand and set my margarita on the table. "Thanks for doing this," I say to my friend.

She stands and walks over to give me a hug. "You're

welcome." Then she whispers in my ear, "I want you two to be happy."

Corey stands and walks over as well. "Where should we go?" he asks me.

I don't want to wait long to talk to him. I want to get everything out in the open. "Let's go sit in my car."

Corey agrees, and we say goodbye to Carson and Chelsea. I put my shoes back on, then we leave.

"So, this is weird," Corey says with a chuckle as we walk to my car.

"Yeah, it is. I'm sorry for the misunderstanding." I unlock my car, and we both get in. "I jumped to conclusions when I saw that selfie on your phone, and it made me feel like I was just another one of your conquests."

"No," Corey interrupts me. "That's not how I think of you at all. I was having the best time with you, and all I could think about was if you'd want to see me again once we got home. When you acted the way you did on Monday, I figured you didn't want to have anything to do with me anymore. I felt as if *you* were just using *me*. Like I was just one of *your* conquests."

Wow. All of this hurt over a stupid misunderstanding? If only I had been more honest about my feelings on Monday. We wouldn't be in this situation right now.

Neither of us says anything. We just look at one another through the darkness. A street light is on just outside my car, so we can see each other well enough. I like Corey. I like him a lot, and I want to keep seeing him. For once in my life, I want to try a relationship. A *real* relationship. I don't want my time with Corey to become some distant memory. I want to make more memories with him, and I hope he feels the same way about me.

Finally, Corey's lips curl up into a smile. "Would you like to go out with me sometime, Brianne?"

His words take my breath away. "Yes, of course I do," I reply.

"Perfect," he says. "Because I like you a lot. I want you to know that."

"I like you a lot, too," I say, and I feel my cheeks blushing. Corey is the only man who's ever made me blush before, and the realization of that makes me happy for some reason.

Corey shifts in his seat, moving closer to me. His hand reaches up and cradles my face. We look into each other's eyes for a moment, and butterflies stir in my belly. I want more with Corey. I want to stop playing games and have something meaningful with him.

He moves in closer and kisses me sweetly on the lips. Instantly, I melt into him. Kissing Corey feels amazing. Being next to Corey feels amazing. I feel different when I'm with him, and I want to see where this goes. We may both be inexperienced in having relationships, but we can figure it out together. There's no one else I'd rather do it with than him.

# *Epilogue*

## BRIANNE

"Oh my God, yes! Right there, Corey! Don't stop!"

Within seconds, my orgasm rips through me, causing my body to shake in satisfaction. Corey doesn't stop fingering my pussy, prolonging the sensations coursing through my body. My hands fly to my breasts, and I rub and pull on my nipples, adding to the pleasure.

"Fuck, you're sexy," he growls as he watches me. "I want to make you come again."

"I want your cock," I say. "I need it."

Corey lines himself up, then slides in nice and slow, taking it all the way to the hilt. My back arches, and I moan at how good it feels. Sex with Corey is unlike anything I've ever experienced before, and I love it. I feel closer to him, and it seems to get better each and every time we do it.

Which is a lot. We have an active sex life.

The past six months have been life changing. I never knew how good it would feel to have someone text or call me throughout the day just to say he's thinking of me or tell me how much he wants me. It gives me a feeling of true happiness I've never felt before. Sure, being wanted by a guy who wanted to have sex with me always felt good and reassuring, but it always left me with an empty feeling. Corey makes me feel special... important... *loved.*

When he first told me he loves me only a month into our relationship, it took my breath away. I'd never been told that by a man before. Since I'd never experienced being in love, I wondered if the strong feelings I had for Corey *was* in fact love, and as soon as he said those three little words to me, I knew it was. We've been happily in love ever since.

"Are you close?" Corey asks, pumping in and out, hitting that spot deep inside that's about to set me off.

"Yes. Right there..." He keeps moving at the perfect pace, and like always, he makes me come so easily.

"I want to come with you," he says, pumping harder. "Tell me when."

That tingly feeling builds, and my body shakes. "Now!" I call out as I come again.

Corey grunts, then calls out as he comes inside me.

As we lie together in bed, my head on his chest and his arm around my shoulder, I feel completely sated. I can't imagine anything better than this. I hear Corey's heart beating in his chest, and I notice my heart is beating in sync with his.

"You should move in with me," his deep voice interrupts the thumping I'm focused on, and his words make me freeze.

*Did he really just say we should move in together?*

I don't know what to say. "What?" Maybe I misunderstood him.

"I mean, you're always over here anyway. It's like you

already live here, but you keep all of your stuff at your apartment."

I sit up and look at him. "Are you serious?"

Corey shrugs. "I like having you here. It would be more convenient for you than having to drive home to get a change of clothes all the time."

I'm speechless. Corey wants to live with me. This is next level relationship stuff, and I've never lived with a guy before. But he's right––I spend all of my time here at his place. When I'm not at work or hanging out with friends, I'm here. I sleep here all the time. In fact, I can't remember the last time I slept in my own bed. Do I want to live with Corey? That question is easy to answer because we're practically living together already.

But this is a big step.

"Are you sure?" I ask, wanting to make sure Corey knows what he's saying. "I mean, I snore sometimes. I can be a little messy. What if we don't get along as roommates?"

Corey touches my arm and smiles. "Babe, I'm completely sure. I've been thinking about this for a while now, I just didn't know when the right time would be to bring it up. Lying here together right now, I figured I'd finally just go for it and ask you."

Again, I'm speechless. I can't believe this is happening right now.

"I *know* you snore sometimes," he continues. "I'm the one who informed you of that fact, and it doesn't bother me. I also know you can be a little messy, but I don't care. It's not as if you're a fucking hoarder." We both laugh. "Are you really worried we won't get along as roommates? We're pretty much roommates already, and we get along fine. Great, actually. I love you, Bri."

My heart melts. Everything he says is true, and it does make sense. We *have* been living together for a while now, just not officially. Why shouldn't I move in with him? I can't think of a single reason not to.

"Okay," I say. "Let's do it! I'll move in with you." Corey smiles wide as he sits up, wrapping his arms around me in a hug.

"I'm so glad you said yes," he says against my neck. "I love you so much."

"I love *you* so much," I tell him as we continue to hold one another.

Suddenly, I'm overwhelmed with emotion. Knowing Corey loves me enough to want to live with me is not only heartwarming, but it also tells me just how deep his feelings are for me. It also affirms my own feelings for him. We've come a long way together––from two single, free-living people who wanted nothing to do with relationships––to finding exactly what we didn't know we wanted in a partner, being in a committed relationship, and falling in love. Now, we're going to take the next step and officially move in together. We're done being the players we once were. If someone had told me a year ago how different my life would be right now, I wouldn't have believed them, and that gives me hope––hope for my future with Corey.

*The End*

# Also by C.L. Collier

## Summers in Seaside Series

Summer Magic (Olivia's story!)

Summer Love (A Summers in Seaside and Seasons of Love Crossover)

## Seasons of Love Series

Holly

Summer Love (A Summers in Seaside and Seasons of Love Crossover)

Autumn (coming soon in the Love and Coffee multi-author anthology)

April (coming in 2024!)

## What I Never Knew Series

What I Never Knew

What I Never Knew I Wanted

What I Never Knew I Needed

## Discovering Us Series

Stacking the Deck

Finding Our Rhythm

Worthy of Love

Meant to Be

**The Vagabond Series**

Passion in Paris

Belize Bliss

**The Salvation Society**

Harbor

Visit C.L. Collier's web site

# Hot Vegas Nights

About the Hot Vegas Nights Series:

I hope you enjoyed my book, Playing Vegas, which is part of the shared world Hot Vegas Nights.

Would you like to read all of them? Find them here on Kindle Unlimited.

The Vegas Strip is the gateway to your wildest fantasies. Where debauchery rules and depravity runs rampant. Elusive billionaires, celebrity bad boys, tantalizing dancers, master mixologists, and sexy tattoo artists are all within reach.

During these 15 Hot Vegas Nights, you'll take a chance on love, lose yourself in entertainment, and gamble your heart away!
　　Fifteen books all written with your pleasure in mind.

Vegas Baby by Melanie A. Smith

Vegas Prince by Mckenna James

Vegas Showdown by Amy Stephens

Healing in Vegas by Sydney Aaliyah Michelle

Vegas Reward by Michelle Donn

Playing Vegas by C.L. Collier

What Happens in Vegas by Sabrina Wagner

The Vegas Pitch by Amanda Shelley

Waking up Married in Vegas by Kaylee Monroe

A Vegas Dare by Kate Stacy

Vegas Valet by TL Mayhew

Vegas Redemption by Anise Storm

All's Fair in Love & Vegas by Shannon O'Connor & M Leigh Morhaime

Vegas Storm by D.M. Davis

Vegas Jackpot by E.M. Shue

*Coming Soon from C.L. Collier*

Hopelessly Devoted: A Romance Anthology to Benefit Women's Cancer Research - coming September 7, 2023

Love and Coffee: A Limited Edition Contemporary Romance Anthology - coming September 19, 2023

Let's Get Naughty 2: A Limited Edition Romance Anthology - coming October 24, 2023

Stud Finder: A Limited Edition Romance Anthology - coming February 6, 2024

C.L. Collier's newsletter - Stay tuned for more!

# Acknowledgments

I'd like to thank S.L. Sterling for putting this multi-author series together! Hot Vegas Nights was a fun series to write for, and I'm grateful I had the opportunity to be a contributing author!

I'd also like to thank Amanda Shelley for inviting me to be a part of this collaboration. Not only that, but Playing Vegas connects to my story Summer Magic from the Summers in Seaside Series--which Amanda spearheaded the idea for. Thanks for helping me stay creative (and busy), Amanda!

Lastly, I'd like to thank my better half for all of his support. Thank you for being my cheerleader and encouraging me to write. I love you!

# About the Author

C.L. Collier is a USA Today Bestselling Author who lives in the beautiful Pacific Northwest. She was raised in the Seattle area, and although she lives closer to Portland, Oregon now, she frequently visits the hometown she loves. When she's not writing, you can find her reading, watching her favorite sports teams, spending time with her family, or going to concerts. She likes her music loud, wine and coffee sweet, and her books steamy.

Click here to visit CL Collier's web site!